GALLOWS HUMOR

Carolyn Elizabeth

BELLA
B O O K S
2019

Bella Books, Inc.
P.O. Box 10543
Tallahassee, FL 32302

Printed in the United States of America on acid-free paper.

First Bella Books Edition 2019

Editor: Ann Roberts
Cover Designer: Judith Fellows

ISBN: 978-1-64247-007-9

Acknowledgments

Many thanks to the folks at Bella Books who saw a submission with an odd title and gave it a read, and for believing it had potential. Thank you to Ann Roberts for taking the rough cut and helping me polish it into a book I am proud to share with the world.

Thank you to the readers of my early fan fiction who were quick with the reviews and words of encouragement to always keep writing.

Most importantly, thank you to my wife, Laurel, who told everyone I wrote a book when I was trying to keep it a secret and who laughed at my hysteria and talked me off the ledge when those first edits came back.

To my children, Henry and Grayson, my undying love and gratitude for keeping it real and yelling 'Mom' in my face until I closed my laptop and fixed you a snack and played a game of foosball.

About the Author

Carolyn Elizabeth was born in Canada and moved to the US as a young child. She has lived in Illinois, New York, New Hampshire, Texas, Maryland, and Connecticut before moving back to Canada several years ago.

She now lives with her family in London, Ontario where she has parlayed her education and professional experience in pathology into a satisfying job in tissue banking for research.

When not reading, writing, or dreaming up new characters and the trouble they can get into she can be found goofing around with her children, cuddling with the dogs while binge watching Netflix, and taking afternoons off work to have adult lunch dates with her wife.

This is her very first book.

Dedication

This one is for younger me who had the desire and ideas
but never the discipline or confidence.

CHAPTER ONE

Corey danced on the balls of her feet, her fighting stance relaxed, and grinned around her mouth guard. Her opponent grinned back, rolling her shoulders, as she circled Corey while waiting for her opening.

"Kick her ass, Curtis," a woman called, her voice echoing through the cavernous converted warehouse, now the gym where Corey spent several mornings and evenings a week.

She snorted a laugh, her gaze flicking to the ropes where a few of their other early morning MMA classmates watched with interest. She'd never beaten Rachel, not even come close, despite her height advantage and longer reach.

But today could be her day. Her focus came back to the ring as Rachel moved in on her, snapping off a couple of jabs in her direction. Corey easily danced out of the way.

Rachel taunted her, gleefully dropping her gloved hands. "What you waiting for, Corey?" she garbled around her mouth guard. "I gotta be at work in less than an hour."

Corey's eyes narrowed at the challenge as she stepped in with a sharp, three-punch combination landing two lefts before letting go with a right overhand punch to her head. She realized her mistake too late as Rachel stepped back, blocked her punch with her left arm, locked her arms around the back of Corey's neck in a double-collar tie, and pulled her forward and down with a hard knee to her solar plexus.

Corey dropped to the mat with a grunt as the air was forced from her lungs. She spit out her mouth guard and canted her head up just in time to see Rachel's gloved fist a second before it smashed into her face—hard.

"Oh, shit." Rachel spit out her mouth guard and dropped to the mat next to her. "Cor, are you all right? I tried to pull that punch. I just meant to smack you in the side of your headgear but you turned into it."

"I'm okay." Corey sat back on her heels, sucking in deep lungfuls of air as she prodded her already tender eye with her fingertips.

"Better luck next time, Curtis," someone cackled from nearby.

"You're getting old, Corey," another voice chimed in.

Rachel scowled in their direction. "Bitches," she muttered. "Twenty-eight isn't old."

Corey grimaced. "I'm thirty-three."

"Oh, well." Rachel grinned. "I'll go find you some ice, Grandma."

Corey wiped steam from the mirror and leaned over the sink, prodding the skin around her eye. It was puffy, tender and already discolored, but it wasn't swollen shut. She stepped back and gave herself a once-over, clad only in her briefs and sports bra. Her skin was tight over muscles defined from three or four days a week at the gym. The ink of her full sleeve tattoo on her right arm, a gift to herself for her thirtieth birthday, was still vibrant. Her teeth were straight and white, her eyes clear and blue. Her hair was cut short but trendy—closely cropped around the sides and back and longer and asymmetrical on top to fall rakishly over her eyes or stick up carelessly if she ran her hands through it—so said her stylist. All in all she had no complaints.

Rachel placed a baggie of ice on the sink. "Don't let those skanks get to you, Cor."

"What? No, I wasn't. I was just—"

"They hope they look as good as you when they're your age."

She spun around. "I'm only thirty-three."

"Yeah, that's what I'm saying." Rachel opened her locker and sat on a bench to change. "I mean if we didn't already know we suck in bed together, I'd totally be all over your shit."

"We didn't suck, exactly." Corey laughed at the memory of their one night together five years ago.

She had only recently moved back to the area and started her position at Jackson City Memorial Hospital. She had joined the Women's MMA Warehouse for obvious workout reasons and to meet people. This gym was particularly appealing because it was the only one that didn't have gang showers. She was far from a prude about her body, or anyone else's, but she drew the line at showering in full view of total strangers.

Rachel, a slightly androgynous twenty-something with a Ruby Rose look—black spiky hair, tattoos and a tongue ring out to prove herself to the world and expand her sexual horizons—latched on to Corey, six years her senior, like a spider monkey. After months of flirting and one night of far too many drinks, Corey relented and figured they should, at least, get it out of the way. While they both got what they needed at the time, the sex was more comical than anything and it never came up again. Their friendship, however, was one of the best things Corey had in her life.

"And anyway, you're still stringing along that cool as ice, yet smoking-hot lawyer." Rachel dragged her coffeehouse T-shirt over her head.

"Financial advisor," she corrected. "Wait. What? Stringing along?"

Rachel pulled on cargo shorts. "Don't pretend you don't know how into you she is. You just haven't gotten around to cutting her loose."

She shook her head. "That's not—"

"Oh, yeah?" Rachel eyed her. "When's the last time you took her out? Have you ever even introduced her as your girlfriend? I can't even remember her name. That's how often you talk about her."

"Anna," Corey mumbled. "And I gave her a key to my place."

"Oh, shit." Rachel pulled on her battered Chucks and grabbed her canvas messenger bag out of her locker. "I'm late and hippy-dippy, yuppie, extra skinny, blah, blah, blah lattes won't make themselves."

Rachel pretended to resent her silly barista job, but Corey was one of the very few people who knew Rachel had dropped out of her first year of university and purchased the failing downtown coffee shop, using tuition money and a small business loan. She was smart and savvy, and within a few years, had turned it into the very successful shop it was today with great food and drinks, open mic nights, poetry slams and an occasional women-only speed dating night.

Corey glanced at the clock. It was after eight and she needed to get moving too. "Don't let the hipsters get you down, Rach," she called as Rachel raced out the door. "Oh, and thanks for the ass kicking."

"Anytime."

She laughed and pressed the melting bag of ice to her eye, her smile faltering with Rachel's words about her half-assed relationship of six months still ringing in her ear.

Corey's vintage, blue and white Ford F-100 rumbled into the lower level parking lot of the hospital. She often wondered what people would say if they knew the morgue and food services shared the same loading dock. She more or less kept regular hours, but she was autonomous, didn't punch a time card and her patients were never an emergency. As long as she didn't have a meeting, she considered her start time anywhere between eight and nine in the morning.

She shouldered her way through the door, adorned with the Latin phrase *Mortui Vivos Docent*, the dead teach the living. The small morgue contained a desk, computer, phone, and file cabinet. She headed past the silver walk-in cooler and into the main autopsy suite, where she heard the stainless steel being banged around.

"Jesus, there you are." Cinnamon James, her sort-of and sometimes lab assistant by day and forensic anthropology PhD student all other times, eyed her up and down, impatiently. "Is that what you're going to wear? And what the hell happened to your face?"

She looked down at her usual faded jeans and even more faded beer T-shirt. "Yes, Mom, this is what I always wear." She frowned back at the petite, younger woman, noticing she was pulled together nicely in khaki dress pants and a light blue button-down blouse that made her look marginally older than her twenty-four years. Cin looked like the blond, doe-eyed cheerleader next door and was constantly dismissed and underestimated as a result. Her name didn't do her any favors either. She was, in fact, whip-smart, highly educated and just had yet another paper published in *Forensic Science Quarterly*, which had generated invitations to several professional conferences to speak on her work.

"What's the occasion?"

"It's the beginning of July, Corey," Cin huffed. "You forgot the new residents were coming—"

"Oh, shit." She spun, mouth agape, and stared at the clock as the minute hand ticked toward nine. For those rare meetings in the land of the living, with her boss and any administrative types, she would at least change into scrubs and a lab coat. People found her five-foot-ten height intimidating enough without adding visible tattoos. "You think I have time to change?"

The door banged open to the anteroom. "Right this way, gang. I know it's a little cramped but we're all friends here."

Cin pressed her lips together with a helpless shrug. "Sorry," she mouthed.

Corey dropped her head back in a silent scream, her eyes tightly closed. "Fuck."

She had just enough time to square her shoulders and straighten her expression before Dr. Edward Tweedle, PhD, Director of Resident Education, appeared followed by a gaggle of first-year residents from multiple specialties. "Dr. Tweedle, good morning," she greeted him and gave a nod to the crisp white coats filing in behind.

Tweedle stopped dead, a few residents piling up behind him, as he took in her appearance with unadulterated disapproval, his eyes narrowing and his perfectly coiffed mustache twitching in anger. "How nice of you to take time out of your bar fight to meet with us."

She bit down on her lip and looked away to keep from snarking back, while a few of the residents within earshot nervously snickered and gaped at her.

His program for resident training using deceased scheduled for autopsy was genius, had won awards for the hospital, and been emulated at other institutions. He accepted all the accolades and Corey oversaw the training. He needed her and he knew it. She considered it job security, but they mutually despised one another.

"I'm assuming you have an appropriate body and the required consents?" he asked haughtily.

She stiffened, opened her mouth to speak but paused too long, unsure of the answer.

Cin jumped in, waving a stack of forms. "Yes, sir. Of course."

His expression relaxed somewhat. "Very good. Thank you, Miss James, for your professionalism and attention to our program. You are a great asset."

Corey smoothed her expression again. "Do you have their paperwork and schedule?" she asked, making a point to fix her gaze on his forehead. She expected much of his animosity stemmed from being three inches shorter than she and having a surname ripe for lifelong bullying.

He thrust a clipboard into her hands. "Make sure they're done in time for grand rounds," he snapped, before pushing his way back through the residents to the door.

Corey turned away from the residents and shot a look to Cin. "Thank you. Will you get the body?" Cin threw on a lab coat and snapped on gloves before making her way through the living bodies to get the dead one from the cooler.

For a brief moment Corey considered putting on a lab coat, but it didn't seem important now. The residents waited quietly with a mixture of expressions—anxious, excited, bored, overwhelmed, and exhausted.

"All right, let's get started. For those of you who don't know, I am Corey Curtis, Autopsy Services Coordinator under the direction of our forensic pathologist, Dr. Randall Webster. I assist Dr. Tweedle with supervising the practicum for your initial weeks of training."

She paused and gave a cursory glance to the information on the clipboard. It was little changed from the past three years. There were twelve residents, four each from the emergency department, general surgery, and medicine. "For the next six weeks I'll be seeing you once a week to practice a few common procedures including central lines, intubations, and arthrocentesis." She paused when she heard the banging of the gurney through the cooler door as Cin made her way back. "Can everyone back up a little?"

It was a small autopsy suite brightly lit with overhead fluorescent lights, and despite the constant powerful ventilation, it always smelled of blood, chemicals, and cold flesh—sometimes overwhelming and rotten depending on the case. There was only one stainless steel table with attached sink, water, suction, and spray attachments. The surface of the table consisted of removable steel grates that allowed fluids and tissue to drop through to the smooth steel surface underneath, slightly slanted toward the sink for efficient cleanup.

One side of the room was lined with counters and cabinets for supplies and the fireproof cabinet for chemicals. The back wall contained a stainless steel dissection bench with attached sink for individual organ examination, a quantity of formalin for preserving tissue, and a scale for weights. The white-tiled floor sloped slightly toward the center drain and could be bleached and hosed down easily.

The third wall held a large whiteboard, one half of which was permanently marked with organ names, a column for weights, and space to write any other observations. The other half of the whiteboard showed a sexless outline of a human body for noting the external examination findings from scars and tattoos, eye and hair color, and external injury and perimortem interventions.

Cin skillfully pushed the gurney through the crowd and lined it up flush with the autopsy table. The body was large and wrapped in several white sheets from the top of its head and tucked under its feet.

"Thanks, Cin." Corey smiled and gave Cin her introduction. "This is Cinnamon James. She works with me here and you'll be seeing her around on occasion. When not giving me a hand, she's studying forensic anthropology at the university under Dr. Audrey Marsh."

Corey moved to the opposite side of the autopsy table and leaned toward the body, using her full height and arm span. She gripped the sheet at the shoulders and knees. She heard the door open and bang closed and straightened to see who was coming in.

The woman moved smoothly into the room and slipped in behind the residents to stand at the back. Corey was positively awestruck as she took her in. She was tall, maybe only an inch or two shorter than Corey, her trim body accentuating amazing curves beneath her stylish clothes. Her skin was naturally bronze and flawless with full lips framed perfectly by gold-highlighted auburn hair in a riot of curls that swept off her face and cascaded past her shoulders. She was beautiful in a way Corey could only describe as otherworldly.

Corey wasn't even aware how long she stared until her gaze swept up to meet the woman's eyes and a single, perfect brow arched in amusement, a smile hinting at her lips.

Corey cleared her throat feeling her face flush. She attempted to hide her embarrassment as she pulled the body across in one strong movement. She gave a nod to Cin, who had clearly seen the entire brief interaction and was fighting a laugh, to begin unwrapping the body.

"I'm not sure how much Dr. Tweedle explained about this practicum but I'll give you a brief sketch. We use bodies of folks whose families have requested autopsies, but for whom a postmortem would otherwise not be required." She stopped when a hand shot up. "Yes?"

"What's the difference between requiring one and requesting one?" an impossibly young-looking woman asked.

"Oh, okay."

She didn't usually get questions about autopsy procedure but she was happy to answer. Her eyes flicked to the woman at the back who was watching her with interest, and she became hyper aware of herself—her too-low voice, and what she must look like, dressed as she was and sporting a shiner.

"Autopsies are required by law for any suspicious death, anyone who has died at home of unknown causes, suicides, and accidents, and all kids all the time, regardless of situation." She glanced around at the faces to see they all, for the most part, seemed interested. "In hospital deaths, what we call "house cases," autopsies are required if the patient dies within twenty-four hours of admission or if they were under direct physician care at the time, for example during surgery or in the emergency department. In these cases the costs are covered and there are no restrictions on the autopsy."

She took a breath. "Next of kin can request an autopsy on a family member who dies but does not meet the requirements for a mandatory post. These can be full autopsies or partial—head only, chest only, whatever—depending on what they want to spend and what information they are looking for. Sometimes the family just wants to know more about how they died. Some family think, usually erroneously, that they have a malpractice case, or they want information on possible heritable conditions and that kind of thing. The expense for those posts is covered by the requesting family members. So, just to bring it around full circle…"

She picked up the chart off the now unwrapped body of a yellow-tinged, older man and flipped through the first couple of pages. "Mr. Wicker, eighty-three, terminal for non-alcoholic end stage liver disease died in hospice over the weekend. Though it's not necessary, his family would like a post to get some more information on his liver disease. As part of the consent we explain we would like to use his body in training minimally invasive procedures and we knock a few bucks off the cost." She looked around. "Make sense?"

Her mystery woman gave a small shrug and nod as if in answer and Corey's lip twitched into a smile. Her belly did a little excited flip at the woman's continued attention.

Corey tossed the man's chart on the counter and referred back to her clipboard. "We don't have a lot of time so let's get started on subclavian central lines." She looked around the room and the faces grew anxious again. "Who here knows what they're doing?"

The room grew uncomfortably quiet save for the sound of shifting weight and shuffling feet as nervous glances shot across the room to each other.

She sighed. "All right, listen." This happened every year on the first day. Her gaze was again drawn to the woman in the back, whose eyes glittered with amusement and offered what Corey interpreted as an encouraging smile.

She found herself mesmerized and worked to break herself from the woman's gaze, clearing her throat. "I am not a doctor. I'm not here to judge you and I don't even know how to do what you do, though I can probably answer your questions about anatomy. I'm here to provide you with an opportunity to learn something before you have to do it on a real live sick person." She glanced around the room and had their full attention. "You are doctors now and are going to be expected to show some confidence and skill in your craft, and more than likely, save someone's life. Fake it till you make it if you have to but take advantage of this time so your next patient doesn't become my patient because of something you did or didn't do." She gestured to the body. "Mr. Wicker is way beyond caring about your technique, and you're not going to hurt him so I suggest you get to work."

The residents immediately grouped together by their department and went over to the three sets of trays Cin had set up for them on the counter, eagerly chattering as they identified instruments and anatomical landmarks.

Corey stepped out of the way, hearing the door open in time to see the woman slip out without saying a word. She frowned, glancing down at her list of twelve names and quickly counting twelve heads. She didn't know who she was or why she had been here and was likely not going to find out now.

"Aw, that's a shame." Cin bumped her shoulder. "Thought you two had a shared moment there for a second."

"Shut up." Corey breathed a laugh, her face heating again. "You don't know who that was, do you?"

CHAPTER TWO

Thayer Reynolds leaned over the desk at the Emergency Department nursing station. "Psst."

Dana Fowler, the head nurse, looked up from her chart. "Hey, you." She smiled at her friend. "You're not on shift for a couple more days. What are you doing here?"

"Hey, Dr. Reynolds," a young second-year resident grinned stupidly at her as he walked by.

Thayer turned and sketched him a wave, as he crashed into a closed sliding door, too busy looking at her to notice where he was going.

"Does that ever bother you?" Dana asked.

"What?"

"Gawkers." She leaned closer. "There are at least three other people stealing glances at you right now."

"Guess I've gotten used to it." Thayer laughed. "It's harmless and anyway there's not much I can do about where people put their eyes." She shrugged. "In answer to your first question about why I'm here, I have meetings and paperwork all week and was in the neighborhood. Do you have time for a coffee?"

Dana glanced at the clock and then at the waiting room and finally at the whiteboard listing which patients were in what curtain being seen by which doctor. "I can go as far as the nurses' lounge, but our coffee is pretty good." She hopped out of her chair and motioned for Thayer to follow her.

Dana eyed her friend over the top of her paper cup. "So, you want to tell me why you're really here?"

Thayer fought a smile and shrugged as she picked at the rim of her cup. "I've been hearing from some of the junior residents about their practicum training in the morgue and what it was like to work down there."

"Aha. I see." Dana grinned, knowingly.

"Aha, you see what?"

"You've been hearing stories of the Valkyrie?" Dana laughed. "I wondered how long it would take you to check her out."

"I wasn't checking her out," Thayer scoffed. "With a nickname like that I was just curious. Does she mind that the residents call her that?"

"I have no idea." Dana shrugged. "But who would mind being named after a Norse warrior goddess?"

"Actually, Valkyries weren't warriors themselves but chose who lived and died on the battlefield, kind of like a Norse grim reaper. They would bring the slain up to Valhalla." Thayer offered. "But I guess it's still an apt nickname."

"Uh-huh. You are such a nerd." Dana grinned at her. "And what did you think?"

"I think the practicum program is a fantastic training tool."

"Give me a break, Thayer." Dana laughed. "What about Corey Curtis?"

Thayer pursed her lips, fighting a smile at the mere mention of the woman's name. "She's definitely intriguing and striking."

"You always did go for the bad girls."

"What makes you think she's a bad girl?" Thayer cocked her head. "Do you know her?"

"No, not at all. I've interacted with her when I need to, but she intimidates the hell out of me and I don't intimidate easily."

"Really?" Thayer said, surprised. "I didn't get that at all from her."

"I'm not the only one, either. She sends a lot of the junior staff scurrying when she comes around."

"Huh." Thayer pursed her lips. "She's definitely a lesbian?"

Dana barked a laugh. "You're joking, right?"

She shrugged, sheepishly. "Well, you know, she could just be sporty or something."

"I suppose. I've always thought she looked like that Olympic swimmer, you know the woman ten years ago who was the oldest to medal? Dara something."

Thayer frowned a moment before the light went on. "I totally know who you mean and she does look like her. She's not gay, though."

"You're killing me, here." Dana laughed at her. "And don't you have other things to worry about besides the sexuality of the morgue, uh, I don't even know what her title is."

Thayer sighed. "Yes, but she's far more attractive to think on than the unpleasant woman in HR I have to meet with first thing tomorrow morning."

Dana winced. "Yeah, I know who you're talking about. Okay, then, did the object of your desire get a look at you?"

"Maybe." Thayer shrugged noncommittally but she could almost feel Corey Curtis's heated gaze. "And it's not desire, it's um, distraction or interest."

"Uh-huh." Dana finished her coffee and tossed the cup in the trash.

"Hi, Dr. Reynolds." One of the junior nurses, right out of school, breezed into the lounge, batting her lashes and putting a little more swing in her hips as she crossed to the locker rooms. She was cute in a pixie-ish, early twenty-something sort of way.

"Hey, um…" Thayer faltered.

"Jules Archer," Dana whispered.

"Jules." Thayer called to the closing locker room door. "Shit."

"Don't worry, hon." Dana laughed. "It's only been a week and you'll learn them all soon enough. Meanwhile they only have one name to learn, and you, my dear, are far more memorable than most of the knuckleheads around here." She glanced at the door then eyed Thayer. "I'm pretty sure Jules is engaged to a man, but apparently your milkshake brings all the boys and the girls to the yard, I guess."

* * *

Corey kicked the door to her condo closed with her heel, pulled the mail from between her teeth and dropped it on the kitchen counter with her keys, phone, and sunglasses. It was past seven before she finally got out of there. After the residents finally left, she still had to do the post on Mr. Wicker and write up the preliminary autopsy diagnoses to send to Dr. Webster. "Hey, Anna are you here?"

They were exclusive. They had agreed on that much, but they didn't live together though Anna had a key and often stayed over. Corey had only been to her apartment downtown a couple of times because Anna didn't have visitor parking. She kicked off her shoes and beelined to the fridge for a beer. She paused, frowning into the fridge, before pulling out the one with the note taped to it. Whatever this was, it was probably not good. She opened the beer and took a long drink before pulling off the note with a deep sigh.

My parents are only in town for one night. You are an asshole.

She stared stupidly at the note for a long minute. "Oh, fuck." She glanced at the clock and then at her watch as if expecting it to say something different. She had assured Anna she would be out in time to meet them for dinner. That was at six and it was now close to eight.

Corey grabbed her phone, swiping it on, to see she had five unread texts and one voice mail. She cringed, sucking air between her teeth as she drained the rest of her beer before starting with the texts.

The first two were irritated, the next two ramped up to worried, and the final one ended with explosively and profanely angry words. She shuffled back to the fridge for another beer and collapsed onto the sofa before daring to listen to the voice mail. The message played for several seconds before Anna spoke. She no longer sounded angry, just sad and resigned.

"I was worried when you didn't show up, so I left my parents at the restaurant and drove by the hospital. Your truck was still there and I knew you just forgot. I left the note on the way back to the restaurant and cleared out my things. There wasn't much. I'm not an idiot, Corey, and I won't be treated like one. I deserve better. The signs have been there for a while, but I just didn't want to see them. Don't call me. I don't need or want to be wooed back and I wouldn't believe you anyway. You are an honorable woman, Corey, and you have behaved dishonorably. I know how that will eat at you. I hope you find her, Corey, and I hope you treat her better. We had some fun times and the sex was good so not a complete waste of my time. Your key is by the coffeemaker."

She let her phone fall to her lap and finished her second beer in several long swallows as she decided how she felt. She was sorry she hurt Anna. She totally agreed the asshole moniker was well deserved. Beyond that, though, she was having a hard time mustering up an emotion for a relationship in which she was never really invested. The sex had been pretty good. She would miss that.

On paper she and Anna ticked all the compatibility boxes yet there was still something missing—something indefinable and essential. She was not a serial dater and by her third beer had nearly convinced herself to take six months off and get her head out of her ass. By her fourth beer she was certain another lover wouldn't be so much a rebound as a do-over. The fifth bottle went unfinished and all the women in her disjointed dreams had auburn hair.

CHAPTER THREE

Corey woke up late, mildly hungover, with a savage cramp in her neck. Then the morning just got worse. She was out of coffee, had to use paper towels for toilet paper and took a cold shower since the hot water heater was having a bad day.

By the time she rumbled into work, her mood was foul and still on the decline. Cin was on campus all day and unavailable to help or talk her out of her rage spiral. She only made it as far as her desk before flopping into the chair with her head in her hands.

It wasn't the end of her relationship that bothered her but how she had been exclusively at fault by being an apathetic jerk and then a coward about ending it. Anna put in all the emotional labor, called her out on her shitty behavior and left with class and dignity intact.

The buzzer sounded from the loading dock. She dragged herself to her feet, feeling like she weighed a thousand pounds, most of that disappointment and guilt, to let in the funeral home to pick up the late Mr. Wicker.

"What's up, Corey?" asked Jude, the twenty-eight-year-old assistant funeral director and son of Mr. Weatherly of Weatherly's Funeral Home. He wrestled the gurney with the non-offensive, faux red velvet body cover through the door.

"Jude," Corey said by way of greeting.

"Whoa." He stopped. "What happened to your face?"

"Oh, yeah." She touched her eye. The swelling had all but disappeared leaving behind a slashing bruise around her eye in a spectacular shade of purple. "I'll get your guy."

"What? That's all I get?" he called as she disappeared into the cooler. "What does the other guy look like? Probably a bloody pulp, huh? Did he try to grab your ass?"

She stood in the cooler, hands on hips, staring at the bloodstained wrapping over a new body she knew nothing about and without accompanying paperwork. "What the shit is this?" she muttered.

"I don't get paid by the hour, Corey," Jude yelled.

"Yeah, yeah," she grumbled as she double-checked the toe tag on the only other body. She wheeled Mr. Wicker out and helped Jude transfer and load his body. She didn't think her mood could worsen, but a department sending down a body without a chart and proper identification was going to send her over the edge.

Jude signed the transfer paperwork. "So, you're not, like, in an abusive relationship or anything, right?" he asked in an uncharacteristic moment of seriousness. "Because I know people."

"What? No, of course not." She would have laughed had he not looked sincerely worried about her.

"Oh, okay." He seemed almost disappointed he couldn't come to her rescue.

She leaned against the doorframe. "The other guy is a twenty-seven-year-old woman in my MMA class named Rachel. She's super cute and real hard-core. She works at the coffee shop downtown with the giant mug on the sign."

"Oh yeah. I know it."

"Go look her up."

He grinned, lopsidedly, flashing a dimple. "Yeah, okay, maybe I will." He seemed to consider for a moment. "Should I mention you?" He gestured to her eye. "Or will that get me a scalding coffee to the balls?"

She laughed. "We're friends. It was an accident. You can mention me." Rachel had never expressed a sexual preference and Jude might just interest her.

Jude had managed to relieve her funk for the moment, and she stabbed at the blinking message light on the office phone and put it on speaker while she massaged her temples. "Please call Sergeant James Collier, Jackson City Police Department, at your earliest possible convenience and arrange a time for the postmortem of the construction site victim from last night," the disembodied, disinterested female voice recited as if she were reading a script.

"Great." Corey scowled at the phone and marched back to the cooler where her scowl morphed into a seething mask of rage as she ripped the sheet off the body. "Jesus Christ."

The head of the man, clearly the construction site victim, was a misshapen, bloody mess with one eye bulging from the socket and his handlebar mustache askew from multiple facial fractures. He was still in his clothes and boots. She assumed DOA and the police brought him in until she caught the flash of white plastic at his wrist. He was wearing a hospital ID tag, so he must have come in with vitals for a hot second and died in the emergency department. She could barely lift his arm because of the intense rigor. She read the name, Gordon Akers.

Now she was really pissed. The kind of pissed a phone call couldn't handle as she slammed the cooler door and snatched the lab coat off the back of her chair fully intending to vent her anger on the first available warm body.

Thayer leaned against the admission desk in the ED, enjoying the hustle and bustle of her new department, while she waited for Dana to get off the phone. She turned at the sound of the receiver hitting the cradle.

"I see you survived HR," Dana mused.

"Barely." Thayer sucked in a sharp breath. "Talk about an intimidating woman."

"Speaking of intimidating women…" Dana's eyes jerked past Thayer to movement over her shoulder.

Thayer followed her gaze as Corey Curtis stalked into the department looking like a storm about to break, her eyes tracking the staff members nearest her until they landed on the unsuspecting Jules Archer passing by. She stepped in front of her to get her attention and motioned her out of earshot of other staff and patients but still in visual range of the desk.

"Wonder what that's about? Do they know each other?"

"Not as far as I know." They watched Corey tower over the young nurse, her body and voice controlled but she was clearly speaking in anger. Jules was shying away from her and looking very uncomfortable. Dana said, "I better go see what's going on."

"May I?" Thayer eyed her friend.

Dana stifled a laugh and grandly gestured in the direction of the two women. "By all means."

"I don't have time for this shit," Corey growled at Jules. "Find it. I'll wait."

Thayer caught the tail end of their conversation and interrupted politely. "May I be of some help?"

"Oh, Dr. Reynolds," Jules said, relieved. "Um, Corey was looking for a chart for a man who died last night. He's in, um, the morgue without paperwork and I just came on and I don't know—"

"It's okay, Jules." She smiled gently at the stammering woman before her eyes moved to Corey Curtis, who stood, arms crossed, her previous glower faltering into something more akin to embarrassment and no small amount of surprise. "I'll take care of it."

Jules disappeared without another word and she faced Corey full-on. "You're scaring the children."

Corey's lips parted in surprise and she rocked back slightly. "I didn't mean to."

"Didn't you?" Thayer allowed herself a small smile.

"I need a chart," Corey blurted.

"So, I gather." She nodded, her eyes flashing with humor. "Let's start there. Whose?"

"Akers, Gordon." Corey cleared her throat and squared her shoulders. "I already have the police calling me about the case and I have no information."

Her voice was so low and smooth Thayer could practically feel it. "I'm not familiar with it by name, but this is what I can do for you. I will find the chart and bring it down to you within a half hour. How does that sound?"

Corey blinked. "That's fine. Thank you," she managed before she stalked out the way she came.

Thayer walked back to the nurses' station meeting Dana's rapt expression with a wide grin. She leaned across the desk and thumbed through a stack of charts so high they were in danger of tipping over. *Akers, Gordon* was near the bottom and she worked it free without upsetting the entire pile. Thayer grinned at her friend. "I need this."

Dana eyed the name on the chart. "Oh yeah. Poor soul died gruesomely last night and…" Her eyes flicked to where Corey had been standing. "Oh, shit. That should have gone with the body. That's what her panties were in a bunch about, huh?"

Thayer leaned back against the counter with the chart tucked under her arm. "I don't know. She doesn't really strike me as the panty type. I'm thinking boy shorts."

"Oh, really." Dana smirked. "And I suppose you think you're going to get into her pants and find out?"

Thayer arched a brow. "No need to rush things." She tapped the chart on the counter. "First things first. Coffee."

Corey walked the stairs back to the basement in a daze, having no idea what had just happened. That woman, Dr. Reynolds, had eyes so light brown they looked golden, and her smoke and whiskey voice made the hair on Corey's arms stand on end. She went up there, guns blazing for that chart, and mere seconds with Dr. Reynolds left her a stammering fool, leaving without her chart and feeling like she'd just done three shots of tequila.

She gave herself a mental shake as she dropped back down into her desk chair to make her phone calls, letting the powers that be know she had a potentially suspicious death case starting in a half hour. She had no doubt the chart would show up in plenty of time.

CHAPTER FOUR

Corey spread a clean green towel onto the wheeled, stainless steel tray and began lining up her instruments—scalpel handle, a sheet of #60 dissecting blades, her favorite tungsten-carbide blunt-tipped scissors, rib shears, calipers, serrated forceps, bone mallet, and skull breaker. She had already changed into scrubs and booties and was replacing the blade on the Stryker bone saw when the door from the hallway opened.

She watched Dr. Reynolds approach, a coffee in each hand, a folder tucked under her arm, and an air of polish and confidence that set Corey's heart racing. She was so caught off guard at their earlier interaction she failed to really see her. The woman was stunning in a khaki pencil skirt and emerald green button-down blouse with understated gold jewelry and very little makeup. Her hospital-issued white coat, shapeless on everyone else, seemed to enhance her figure.

Corey was determined to show a little class herself, or at the very least, not make an ass out of herself again. "Is one of those for me?"

"Yes." Thayer handed her a coffee. "I thought perhaps you could use one, and I'm afraid I haven't made a very good first impression." She reached into the pocket of her coat and produced an array of cream and sweeteners.

"No, thank you." Corey waved them off. "Black is good, thanks."

"Of course." Thayer's mouth quirked as she looked her over. "I'm Thayer Reynolds. I'm sorry I've not managed to introduce myself yet." She extended her hand.

Corey, thankful she hadn't yet touched anything that required her to first wipe her hands on her pants, gripped her hand—warm, strong, with long, elegant fingers and neat, unadorned nails—and hoped she didn't hold it for longer than was appropriate. "Corey Curtis."

"I enjoyed your resident class yesterday." Thayer smiled. "You seem to have made quite an impression and some of them are still talking about you. I assume you know what they call you?"

"I do." She rolled her eyes. "It could be worse."

"Oh, indeed." Thayer laughed. "You could be T-Rex or Jugs or Wheezer and those are just a few of the ones I've heard. I don't even know who those people are yet."

"Jugs is a man, by the way, and the name doesn't have anything to do with his body." The door opened again. She looked past Thayer and gave a nod. "And here comes Wheezer now."

A morbidly obese man with a ruddy face and a thinning, gray comb-over shuffled into the anteroom and lowered himself into the desk chair, unleashing a groan of plastic and metal. He physically had to pick his own leg up and position it across his knee. His breath came in panting gasps as he attempted to don the shoe covers.

Thayer winced. "Oh, my."

"Dr. Randall Webster, forensic pathologist. It's best if you just don't watch."

Thayer eyed her. "Is he all right?"

Corey shrugged. "You're the doctor."

"Yes, and if someone came into my department looking and sounding like that I'd probably be admitting him for a full workup," she said grimly.

Corey arched a brow. "You don't sound like a resident." She took a chance that Thayer Reynolds was indeed flirting with her and let her gaze wander the woman's body. "You don't look like one either."

Thayer's brows rose. "What do I look like?"

"Oh, hello." Dr. Webster lumbered into the room before Corey had a chance to answer, his eyes boldly assessing Thayer. "You must be the new emergency department fellow, Tracy Reynolds?" He held out his hand.

"Thayer Reynolds." She corrected him with a dazzling smile and shook his hand. "It's very nice to meet you, Dr. Webster. Corey speaks very highly of you."

"Oh?" His gaze flicked to Corey in surprise. "That's always nice to hear. Are we just about ready to get started?"

"We're just waiting for Sergeant Collier." Corey glanced at the clock. "He should be here any minute."

He glanced around. "Right. Right. Do you have the chart?"

"Right here, sir." Thayer held it out.

"Thank you, my dear." He opened the folder and flipped through the few pages. "Ghastly business. Was he your patient?"

"Oh. No, sir. I don't start in the rotation for another day."

"Well, we're happy to have you on staff, Tracy." Dr. Webster lumbered back toward the desk with the chart.

"He's charming." Thayer rubbed the fingers of her right hand together. "And really sweaty."

"You think that now." Corey laughed. "Come back in a few hours."

"Is that when you'll be through?" she asked.

"I, uh, no, I meant—"

"I know what you meant." Thayer smiled. "I guess I was just hoping for the opportunity to get to know you better. I haven't even had the chance to ask you what happened to your eye." She reached up, lightly brushing her fingertips down the side of Corey's face.

"I'm, uh, it was—"

The door banged open again. "Where's this goddamn body, Curtis?" Sergeant James Collier stalked in, nodding to Dr. Webster in the anteroom briefly.

"Am I interrupting?" the sergeant asked from the doorway as he looked between them.

Corey cleared her throat and focused her thoughts. She had been hit on before, plenty of times, but never by someone like Thayer Reynolds—smart, bold, charming, and bewitchingly beautiful. Corey didn't know which way was up right now and she needed to get her head on straight. "Uh, yeah, I mean no, not interrupting." She cleared her throat again. "Sergeant James Collier, this is Dr. Thayer Reynolds, the new ED Fellow."

"Jim." Collier extended his hand. "Good to meet you, Dr. Reynolds."

Thayer shook his hand. "Thayer is fine. It's nice to meet you, Jim." She turned briefly back to Corey. "I guess I'll get out of your way."

Jim Collier was a big man, well over six feet and barrel chested from years of working out. He had short, salt-and-pepper hair and a thickening middle from too much beer, but he was still fit and good looking for a man pushing fifty despite his dated suits and crooked ties. He was gruff, profane, and rough around the edges, but he also had a huge heart. Corey thought he was an excellent cop, which one didn't need to be to know something was going on between Thayer and Corey. "Leaving so soon?" he asked Thayer's retreating form and eyeing Corey from the side.

"Not my circus, not my monkeys." Thayer looked back over her shoulder and threw Corey a wink.

He waited until the door closed behind her before he grinned at Corey.

"What?" she snapped.

"You are so going to fuck that up, Curtis. That woman is way out of your league." He snorted a laugh. "Which reminds me, has that pretty little banker kicked you to the curb yet?"

She sighed heavily and ran her hands through her hair.

"Oh, shit." His mouth gaped. "She did, didn't she?"

"Last night." She might as well say it out loud.

"She do that to your face too?"

"What? No." She scowled. "It was an accident at the gym."

"Keep telling yourself that."

CHAPTER FIVE

"Make sure you get pictures of his head," Collier rumbled as he flipped open his notebook.

Corey's eyes flicked to him. "Yeah, thanks, Collier." She crouched at the top of the victim's head, snapping photos with their high-resolution digital camera. Dr. Webster guffawed from his perch so far away she wondered why he wasted the energy putting on booties. The body would have to explode for him see any blood. She took pictures from every angle, standing on a stool and stretching to her full height, arms extended, to get full shots looking down.

Setting the camera down, she donned her gown and plastic apron. She pulled a bonnet over her hair and settled a face shield over that. Finally, she worked a second pair of extended cuff gloves over the ones she already wore and snapped them over the cuffs of her gown to prevent blood from leaking into the sleeves of her gown.

She paused between each blood-soaked article of clothing as she removed them—T-shirt, jeans, briefs, belt, socks, boots—to record the description on the whiteboard before bagging them up. "You go through his pockets?"

"Yeah. Nothing exciting." Collier stepped closer to appreciate his injuries. "Je-sus."

There were multiple, gaping lacerations to his scalp, some with visible skull protruding. His chest looked caved in on one side and his left leg angled unnaturally. His back and right side were mottled red and white where blood had pooled around the pressure of the ground against his skin where he landed.

"He's got a nicotine patch." She pointed to his left shoulder before taking a picture of it. She noted the faded tattoos on his right forearm and shoulder, an old appendectomy scar, and the missing tip of his left second finger from a long ago healed injury.

"Huh." Collier pursed his lips and jotted a note. "All right, I'll run down what I know."

"We're listening," she encouraged while placing a ruler against one of the scalp lacerations before taking the picture. She had already filled up much of the body diagram on the whiteboard with notes.

"Akers, Gordon. Fifty-six-year-old white male, five-eleven, one hundred eighty-five pounds, married to wife Gloria for thirty-six years. They have two sons—Gordon Jr. and David—thirty-five and thirty-one respectively, both married and living in the city. Worked for Conrad Construction since he was eighteen, worked his way up, been foreman for the last seven years, working on the building going up on Coburn and Hall for the last year. Which, by the way, has kindly shut down while we look into Akers's death. The company says they'll keep it closed through the week since he was well liked and respected."

Corey set the camera down again and moved over to the body. She lifted his torso with her left arm and slid the body block between his shoulder blades so his head dropped back and his chest was thrust up. "How do you know all this already?"

"Because I'm a damn good cop, Curtis."

"Uh-huh." She snapped a scalpel blade on the handle.

"And because he has a public intoxication from five years ago."

She grinned, eyeing him through the shield as she lined up her first incision. She made two swift cuts from each shoulder to sternum, then one down, around the navel to the pubic bone in the classic Y-incision. Collier went on as she started to work on one side and began to flay the layers of skin, muscle and fat away from the ribs and abdominal cavity.

"The guys knocked off at precisely five p.m. because of union policy, and he stayed behind to check their work. They were on the fifth floor, by the way. It's assumed he went for a smoke over the air duct under construction. A lot of guys did if they could get away with it. "

She spread both torso flaps open like a book, exposing the muscle and bone of the rib cage and gripped the triangular section of skin at his neck, going slower now as the skin was much thinner. She pulled it back, teasing off the connective tissue, while being careful not to button hole the neck, breaking the skin and royally pissing off the funeral home that had to fix it, cosmetically. "Went for a smoke, huh?"

"Don't interrupt. He never made it home for dinner. His wife called a friend from the company around eight and a couple of guys went over to the site to look for him. Found him at the bottom of the air duct five stories down. Nobody heard anything and nobody saw anything. Still had weak vitals. Paramedics were called and he was transported here. Time of death called in the ED and Bob's your uncle." He snapped his notebook closed.

She remained quiet as she gripped the rib shears in both hands, snapping through the lateral, intercostal cartilage between the ribs and sternum on each side, then the clavicles. Sweat ran down her back and neck as she pried the wedge-shaped section of chest plate off, spilling blood over the sides, to splatter onto the floor over her feet. She ripped the nicotine patch off his shoulder and held it up.

"I don't know, Curtis. Maybe it was to appease his wife? Maybe it's a year old and he just never took it off?"

"Gross. Was there a cigarette? A lighter?"

"As a matter a fact, there was." He tossed a baggie with a battered chrome lighter and crumpled soft pack of Camels to her. She caught it with a bloody-gloved hand.

He smirked. "These were found with him at the bottom. Keep them here with the clothes until we know what to do with them. Shit gets lost all the time in evidence." He produced another bag with a multipurpose tool, gum and some coins and set it on the counter. "This too."

Dr. Webster wheezed to his feet and ambled over to the body. "Suction please, Corey."

She uncoiled the plastic tubing from beneath the table and turned on the power. Blood filling the chest and abdominal cavity sucked up the tube into a vacutainer underneath the table. "Looks like just about three liters." She switched off the machine and recorded her notes on the whiteboard. The man had exsanguinated half his blood volume into his chest. She couldn't believe he had vitals.

Dr. Webster picked up a long, thin, steel probe and peered into the body. "Rib fractures, punctured lung, liver and spleen lacerations." He poked around with the probe.

He shuffled around to the head and slid blood-soaked clumps of hair away to better see the head lacerations. "Open the head now, please."

She snapped a fresh blade on the scalpel handle and moved to the head of Gordon Akers. She ran her blade across the crown from ear to ear, down to the bone, in order to pry the thick skin of the scalp forward over the face and backward over the skull while allowing the funeral home to reconstruct it with ease and hide the incision. The skull shifted beneath her hands, cracking open like an egg.

Dr. Webster clucked his tongue. "I've seen enough." He moved over to the counter and pulled a blank death certificate from a drawer. "Where are the blue pens?"

She waved her bloody scalpel in his direction. "In the same drawer."

Vital Records required death certificates be filled out in blue pen only so the original could be easily discerned from a photocopy. Also, there could be no mistakes or cross outs or it would be sent back. Nothing put her in a worse mood than chasing down physicians who didn't know how to complete a proper death certificate. As infuriating as Webster could be, she did appreciate his attention to completing paperwork.

He scribbled away for a few minutes. "You can complete the rest." It wasn't a question. "I have a meeting with a prosecutor in an hour to go over my testimony in that hit-and-run from last month." He ambled out, wheezing audibly.

She leaned over the counter, keeping her dripping hands out of the way, to read the cause of death. "Catastrophic trauma to the head and chest due to a fall of five stories." She shrugged. At least it didn't say "cardiac arrest" or "respiratory arrest," neither of which was actually an acceptable cause of death. Everyone died when their heart and lungs quit working. "He left manner of death blank, by the way."

"So?" He was jotting notes and didn't look at her. "That's why you make the big bucks—checking the box marked accident."

"What are you even doing here if you didn't think his death was suspicious?" she snapped. "Why didn't they send me a rookie who has to pretend to answer the phone every five goddamn seconds so they can go out in the hallway?"

"I was available," he said dryly as he tucked his notebook back into his pocket. "And why wouldn't I want to come down here when you're so pleasant?"

"You're not even going to stay?" she yelled as he headed to the door. "Will you, at least email me the scene photos?"

"I'll get right on that," he called over his shoulder sarcastically. "You make autopsies fun, Curtis."

She shook her head, grinding her teeth in frustration. She now needed to complete the autopsy by herself, a task likely to take hours if she was going to document the trauma thoroughly. And she was always thorough, especially in a case that could be going to court, accident or not.

She folded the scalp flap back into place and moved back to the internal organs. She photo-documented the internal injuries documenting sizes and locations of all the pathology she could detect without complete removal of the organs. They would not necessarily ever get sent out, but she took fluids for lab work including blood, urine, and vitreous for a routine toxicology screen if anyone called for it.

There were no surprises, but the list of internal damage was extensive, as one would expect from a fall of more than fifty feet. She bagged up the organs and placed them back into the body cavity for the funeral home to deal with before moving back around to focus on the head.

Despite the fractures, she was still able to get the Stryker evenly around the skull and remove the calvarium—the skull cap. She pulled the bone gently from the adhered brain matter, blood clot, and membranous dura to reveal the brain itself. The convolutions were ragged with blood pooling and clotting around the lacerations. She gently pried the brain up at the frontal lobe with her left hand, the scalpel in her right, skimming along inferiorly, severing the attached nerves, vessels, and spinal cord by feel alone. She eased the brain up and out with two hands, careful not to cause further damage.

She weighed the brain, took more photos and a few tissue sections before adding the brain to the bag of organs. The final photos were of the inside of the skull to document the basilar skull fractures and areas of surrounding hemorrhage.

The bagged organs were sewn into the body cavity, the broken limbs straightened, and blood sponged from the skin. She eyed the removed part of the skull and decided to see if she could piece it back together. There was no way to singularly characterize the damage. The plate of bone was a mess of chaotic fractures, but as she set the pieces back together, a different pattern began to emerge. An area covering the posterior aspect appeared to form an elongated, depression where the bone was broken inward in the particular shape of whatever the head struck—or was struck with.

She considered the puzzle, flipping a small shard around until it lined up properly, completing the picture. She placed a ruler next to the area and took some more photos. The fracture was about nine centimeters long and barely two centimeters in width. Carefully replacing the calvarium, she folded the skin back over it to keep it in place and added a few quick sutures with the heavy nylon thread. She lined up the skin over the fracture site and studied it more closely. There was a near-full thickness laceration near the crown corresponding to the superior end of the fracture. She took her last photos and set the camera on the counter. It was all over but the cleanup.

CHAPTER SIX

It hadn't been hard for Corey to come up with a reason to visit the ED the next morning. An apology for the young nurse she had barked at yesterday was more than called for. Nevertheless, Corey hesitated outside the stairwell, her stomach jangling with nerves she hadn't felt since she first made a move on Bethany Stills in undergrad. She had changed into scrub pants and a plain long-sleeved black shirt, trying to appear less intimidating.

Thayer Reynolds had quite clearly come on to her. She had nothing to be nervous about. She was the chased not the chaser. Collier's words stuck in her head, though, about Thayer being out of her league and it rattled her confidence right on the heels of the debacle with Anna.

One thing at a time. She shifted the paper-wrapped bottle to her other hand and looked around the busy department for the young woman from yesterday. She was at the admission desk talking with the head nurse, Dana Fowler. Corey had worked with Dana before, liked her even. She had pretty, chestnut hair and big brown eyes. She had always been respectful and helpful to Corey in the past, though their relationship had never gone past professional, not even to friendly.

She took a deep breath, squared her shoulders and strode across the room. "Excuse me."

Both women looked up at her—startled—the younger one's eyes widening in alarm and Nurse Fowler's narrowing in suspicion. If she weren't so nervous she'd have laughed.

"Oh, I gotta run and do that thing," the younger one said.

"Wait." Corey jerked a hand out and stopped just short of touching her. "Jules, right?"

Her gaze darted toward Dana. "Yeah?"

Corey pulled out the bottle of wine she had picked up last night. "I wanted to apologize for being such a jerk yesterday." She held out the bottle. "I was having a rough morning, but I should never have taken it out on you. I'm sorry."

"Oh." Jules's eyebrows shot up and she took the bottle, smiling hesitantly. "Um, thanks. Thank you. It's cool. I'm sorry I couldn't help you."

"No worries." Corey grinned. "It all worked out."

"Jules, they need you in three," another nurse called as he raced by.

"Oh, I gotta hustle." Jules thrust the bottle at Dana. "Can you stash this for me?"

Corey shuffled her feet nervously and glanced around the room while Dana disappeared to hide the bottle beneath the desk.

Dana popped back up. "Something I can help you with, Corey?"

"Oh, um, yeah." She cleared her throat. "I was hoping Thayer, er, Dr. Reynolds was around?"

"She's with a patient in curtain two."

"Right, of course. She's working." Corey hoped she was hiding her disappointment better than Dana was hiding her amusement.

"You want me to pass along a message?"

"No. No message." She suddenly felt profoundly stupid like she was chasing after some girl on the schoolyard. "Thanks, Dana."

Thayer smacked her chart down on the desk in front of Dana. "Man, that guy was chatty."

"Pardon, Dr. Reynolds," a gravelly voice behind her made her turn.

"Good morning…" Her gaze flicked to Dana in a panic.

"Hi, Jerome." Dana winked at her. "Whatcha got?"

The older, grizzled porter held out a cup of coffee toward Thayer in a wobbly hand. "I made an extra cup by mistake. Thought you might like it."

Thayer smiled. "Thank you, Jerome." She took a sip of the bitter brew. "It's perfect."

A rare smile flashed on his face before he shuffled away.

She set the coffee behind the counter. "That was sweet but this tastes like it was made in a mop bucket." She saw Dana eyeing her, curiously. "What?"

"You've got the magic of a unicorn or something." She shook her head. "I've been working here eight years and I don't think I've ever heard that man speak more than one word."

She grinned. "Eh, well, what can I say? It's a gift." Dana continued to stare at her. "What now?"

"I never got a chance to follow up with you yesterday. What happened when you went to drop off the chart in the morgue?"

"Oh, God." Thayer groaned theatrically and covered her face with her hands. "Uh, I may have made a completely inappropriate pass at her practically in front of her boss and the police."

Dana's brows shot up. "Wow. Really?" She laughed. "God, Thayer, I'm sorry about the circumstances but I'm so glad you're here. I really have missed you."

"Happy to entertain. I'll be here all week." She reached for the next chart and flipped it open.

"Well, whatever you did seems to have made quite an impression."

Thayer was only half paying attention as she scanned the intake sheet. "Why? What happened?"

"Corey Curtis was up here a while ago."

Her head snapped up. "She was? Was she looking for me? I mean, what was she doing?"

Dana laughed. "Actually, she was apologizing to Jules with, if I'm not mistaken, a very nice bottle of wine." Dana paused before adding, "And she was looking for you."

Thayer smiled triumphantly.

CHAPTER SEVEN

There were no autopsies scheduled and no residents to train. Corey puttered around the morgue cleaning instruments until they shone, reorganizing and restocking supplies, and doing pretty much anything she could think of to avoid the mountain of paperwork that faced her following yesterday's post—and to keep her mind off Dr. Thayer Reynolds.

The clothes and personal effects of Gordon Akers were still on the counter where she had left them. The police had taken his wallet, keys, and wedding ring to return immediately to his widow and left Corey with the loose change, a folding multi-tool, and a half pack of Nicorette gum in one baggie and the lighter and cigarettes in another, both sitting atop his bagged bloody clothes and boots. She considered where to put them so they went with his body when the funeral home arrived. Bodies were supposed to be picked up within three days, but it wasn't unusual for victims of tragic deaths to hang around for a while until the family had processed what had happened and made arrangements.

She finally decided to put his belongings in the fire cabinet because it was the only storage space that locked. She stacked the items next to the unopened formalin boxes and other flammable chemicals where they would be safe and out of the way. She picked up one of the baggies, fiddling with the items through the clear plastic as she ruminated on why the man was wearing a patch, chewing nicotine gum and still smoking.

"Hey, Corey, what are these photos from?" Cin called from the other room.

"Which?" She placed the items inside and locked the heavy, metal fireproof door before wandering into the other room.

Cin was going through her paperwork on Gordon Akers. "These." She held up the photos of her hastily reconstructed skull as she pawed through the other photos she had printed out for the hard copy of the report. "This is a sweet signature fracture. I could use this for my undergrad forensics class when I teach the segment on blunt force trauma, assault, and determination of weapons. What caused it?"

She leaned against the doorway. "Guy fell down an airshaft at a construction site."

"Oh, bummer." She looked at the photo again, considering. "He hit something on the way down? I could still make it work."

"I guess." Corey shrugged and moved to the computer. "Slide over and I'll see if Collier emailed me the photos of the scene." She opened her email, dismayed at her overflowing inbox of reminders of online safety training courses, which were overdue, her mood recovering when she saw the file from Collier. "Here." She opened the attachment and scrolled through a series of dark, nearly unrecognizable images. If she hadn't known what it was supposed to be, she wouldn't have had a clue.

"These photos are shit," Cin grumbled. "My left tit could take a better picture."

"Oh, yeah?" Corey appraised her breasts. "I'd like to see that."

Cin eyed her mischievously. "Can we take a ride?"

She frowned for a moment before she fully understood what Cin was asking. Corey had no other obligations for the morning and she had to acknowledge her own curiosity about this case. Something wasn't sitting right with her. "I'll get the camera and you get a light."

"What are we going to tell them?" Cin leaned forward and peered through the windshield as Corey pulled her truck up to the site.

"Tell who?" She appraised the building before jumping out of the cab and grabbing the camera. She had changed back into jeans and a T-shirt for their field trip and her truck fit right in at the rutted dirt parking area, though there were no other cars.

"Isn't someone going to ask what we're doing?" Cin grabbed one of the rechargeable high-powered floodlights and followed her out.

"Collier mentioned the site was closed for the week and it may still be an active crime scene so we can just wing it." She slung the camera around her neck. "Over here."

She led the way to the trailer that served as an office and grabbed a couple of beat-up hard hats off hooks by the door. "Put this on so it looks like we know what we're doing."

"It smells like ass." Cin wrinkled her nose. "And it's probably going to give me lice."

"Quit bitching." Corey laughed. "This was your idea."

"Which way?"

They both scanned the area, the ground littered with stacks of lumber, brick, and rebar. A crane and a cement truck were parked at one end of the site while a roll-off dumpster with a refuse chute system leading to the fifth floor sat at the other. The building spanned the entire block and there were several entrances on the ground floor.

"There." Corey pointed to a square cutout in the wall about three feet off the ground, from which a length of yellow police tape flapped in the breeze.

"Oh, good eye." Cin headed to where she indicated. She leaned in and flicked on the light, the entire airshaft lighting up. "Whoa, that fall would do it." She pointed the light to the floor, illuminating a large, dark, and thickly congealed pool of blood. "And it did."

"I'm going in." Corey threw a leg over the edge and eased her tall frame through the small opening, carefully avoiding the blood. "Shine the light up the shaft, Cin."

"Gotcha." Cin leaned in and directed the light through the shaft. It was a smooth sheet of metal as far as the eye could see.

Corey snapped off a series of photos starting at the top and working her way down. "I don't see anything he could have struck on the way down. Maybe he landed on something but there's nothing here now. Could they have moved it?"

"I don't think so." Cin moved out of the way and held the light down as Corey climbed out and took photos of the blood-soaked bottom. "We'd probably see a disruption in the blood pool if there had been an object underneath him that they moved when they found him." She gestured to the unbroken bloodstain.

"Hey," a gruff voice barked.

They both jumped and whirled around to see a large, red-faced man stalking toward them, a cigarette hanging out of his mouth. He looked unkempt, and as he got closer, he smelled of beer and body odor.

"What the hell do you think you're doing here?" He snatched the cigarette from his mouth and flicked it to the ground. "You fucking vultures. What are you, press? Ambulance chasers?" He jabbed a finger at them to punctuate his words.

Corey and Cin shared a glance and both spoke at the same time.

"We're from the hospital."

"We're with the police."

His eyes narrowed and darted to the shaft. "Well, which is it?"

"The postmortem examination and subsequent investigation into Gordon Akers's fatal fall showed some inconsistencies, and we are here to confirm some details about how he died," Corey rambled vaguely

His eyes remained suspicious as he looked her over and then he turned to Cin, his face curling into a grotesque, predatory leer as his gaze lingered on her breasts. "What's your name, girlie? You got some ID?"

Cin paled visibly and stepped back from him, trying to avoid his repulsive gaze.

"We're done here," Corey said.

Corey placed a protective hand on Cin's back, putting herself between the man and her friend as she propelled Cin forward toward the truck. She didn't spend half her week training in mixed martial arts because she ever expected to get into a fight, but she had every confidence that she could use what she had learned effectively to defend herself or anyone else.

"We'll just get out of your way. Sorry for any inconvenience." She hurried them back to the truck, tossing the hard hats on the ground.

They hopped in and locked the doors, but the man had not moved. He watched them for a moment before turning to peer into the airshaft, as if they had left some clue behind. Corey threw the truck in reverse and tore out of the lot in a cloud of dirt.

CHAPTER EIGHT

Corey glanced at Cin as she scrolled through the pictures. "Cin, are you all right?" Her own heart rate was just now returning to normal after their confrontation.

"Fine," she said tightly. "I don't see anything here at all that could have caused that fracture."

"No, I know." She considered her next move. "I should pitch it to Collier and Webster. See if they want to run with it."

"Can you just drop me off on campus?" Cin stared out the windshield.

"Sure. Are you sure you're all right?"

"Yeah, of course." Her laugh sounded forced. "It's not like creepy guys have never stared at my boobs before."

"No doubt." She smiled crookedly at her. "I stare at your boobs all the time."

Cin laughed genuinely this time and punched her in the arm. "Thanks, Corey."

"For what?"

"For being you." She shrugged. "For being willing to get between him and me."

She pulled in front of Cin's building and stopped, looking at her seriously. "There was something off about that guy."

"I know. I could feel it." She gazed at Corey intently.

"What?"

"You make people feel safe."

"What?"

"That's it." Cin grinned, nodding her head. "There's this thing about you. I've never been able to put my finger on until just now. I feel safe with you." She seemed pleased with her revelation. "I mean you're still intimidating as hell in your own way, but yeah, you very much have this protective warrior energy about you."

Corey laughed. "Um, okay, I guess."

Cin leaned across the seat to give her a kiss on the cheek, something she had never done before. "Thanks for looking out for me."

She felt her cheeks flush. "Yeah, no problem."

Corey worked for hours on the preliminary autopsy report for Gordon Akers. It was all straight up just stating the facts, descriptions, weights, measurements, and photos. No speculation and no opinions. She left nothing out and it was thirteen pages long. She forwarded a copy to Dr. Webster and to Collier along with a message about the suspicious fracture and that there was nothing in the scene photos to suggest a cause. She left off the part about visiting the site to take her own scene photos. She hoped one of them would be interested in knowing more so she could pursue it.

She tried not to be disappointed that she hadn't crossed paths with Thayer Reynolds all day. She had even strolled through the cafeteria late in the day, a place she avoided at all costs, in the hopes of running into her. She couldn't come up with another reason to go to the ED and doubted Thayer would have any reason to be in the morgue.

With effort she pushed all thoughts of Thayer out of her head and focused on her evening grudge match with Rachel as she changed into her black compression shorts and black tank in the bathroom adjacent to the morgue. She exited out the back to the loading dock where her truck was parked.

She stopped short when she saw Thayer Reynolds sitting on her tailgate. She must have changed at some point because Corey sincerely doubted she wore ass-hugging, faded jeans and a coral-colored tank top to work. She sure knew how to make a statement. Corey imagined she looked amazing in whatever she wore, or if she wore nothing at all. As fast as she had the thought, her belly clenched. She immediately chastised herself for her impure thoughts and wiped the smile from her face. Thayer hadn't appeared to have heard her come out and she intended to take advantage.

"What are you doing on Dan's truck?" Corey asked as she faced her.

"What?" Thayer jumped up, startled. "Oh, shit." She gently closed the tailgate and looked around nervously.

It was adorable and Corey's face split into an enormous grin.

Thayer eyed her, lips pursed. "Very funny."

"I thought so." She slung her kit bag into the back and turned to lean against the truck, still grinning.

Thayer returned her smile. "Who's Dan?"

Corey shrugged, pleased to find Thayer did not take herself too seriously and could laugh easily at herself. "I have no idea, but you've had me on my heels since we met, and I thought I'd get some payback."

Thayer nodded, a hand raised in agreement. "Fair enough." Her expression sobered and she took a breath. "About that. I'm afraid I owe you an apology for yesterday. I'm not usually so forward and that was not very professional of me."

"No apology necessary. I don't imagine you got where you are by being shy." She let her gaze roam Thayer's body, slowly, letting her know the interest was reciprocal.

"That's true, I suppose." Thayer returned the appraisal. "You're looking particularly sporty."

Corey made a concerted effort not to squirm as her eyes lingered. "I have a class. Well, a fight really."

"Fight?"

"I go to a women's MMA gym."

Thayer's brows raised in surprise. "No kidding." She let her gaze slide over her again coming back to her face. "Guess that solves the black eye mystery."

"Yeah." She huffed a breath. "I can hold my own or beat everyone else, but Rachel just seems to have my number."

"And you're fighting her again?"

"Until I beat her." Corey grinned. "Or until she kills me, I guess."

"That sounds serious." Thayer pressed her lips together. "Maybe you should have a doctor on site."

"Oh, there's always a trainer at the gym..." She trailed off at Thayer's widening smile. "You meant you."

Thayer nodded. "I was going to ask if I could take you out for a drink, but now that you have other plans I'm adapting."

"You mean you want to come and watch?"

"Is that okay? We can get a drink after."

She barked a laugh. "Probably going to need more than one. And lots of ice."

"That can be arranged."

Corey studied her for a moment, trying like hell not to overthink it, before walking around to the passenger side and opening the door. "Right this way."

The silence was anything but comfortable and Corey wondered if Thayer could feel the air crackle between them or if she was the only one affected by their closeness. Her heart skipped when Thayer spoke. Her voice was like foreplay.

"How did you end up in Jackson City, New York?"

"Oh, um, I came to JCU for undergrad to work with Audrey Marsh. She's the forensic anthropologist and does all the skeletal consults for the city. I have an undergrad degree in biological anthropology with a specialization in forensics and paleopathology."

"Wanted to be the next Temperance Brennan?" Thayer smiled at her surprised expression at the question. "I watch TV."

"I prefer the books to the show," she corrected with faux disdain.

"What?" Thayer laughed. "Not into the whole adorkable Zoey whatever her name is?"

"Wrong Deschanel sister." Corey grinned at her. "And, no. I feel about the show *Bones* how you probably feel about *Grey's Anatomy*."

Thayer nodded. "So, you wouldn't believe me if I told you I've actually held a live bomb inside a man's chest cavity to keep if from detonating while someone defused it?"

"Not a chance." She smiled. "I drove around the city once with a human skull in a brown paper bag on the passenger seat and almost hoped I got pulled over so I could say out loud, 'I'm not a sociopath, I'm an anthropologist.'"

"Oh, that would have been amazing. I probably shouldn't tell you about all my trysts in hospital storerooms either," Thayer added, straight-faced.

"Really?" Corey's head whipped sideways and they veered out of their lane.

"Watch the road!" Thayer shouted. "No, of course, not really. I hope you don't think I'm that easy."

She sucked in a breath and clutched the wheel, correcting her driving and glancing at Thayer who looked on the verge of cracking up. Corey figured she should redirect back to the original question before the conversation really got away from her and she made some totally ridiculous comment about wanting to meet her in a storeroom. She inhaled deeply. "Anyway, I was working as the autopsy tech at the hospital part-time, assisting Dr. Webster while I was in school. We worked well together and he was thrilled to have someone to do the wet work. When I was waffling about getting my PhD, he suggested an MS in pathology and certification as a pathologists' assistant. He arranged it so the hospital would subsidize my master's degree if I would come back and oversee autopsy for them in a more advanced capacity."

"So, you gave up the dream?" Thayer asked seriously.

She sighed. "Yes and no, I guess. I read this comment online, I don't even remember where. What kind of world would we live in where there was a high demand for people to identify skeletal remains? Pretty bleak, I guess. The world is bleak enough so it's not a bad thing that there isn't a call for more people to recover bodies full time. So my future would have been academia and consulting, and I couldn't really see myself in school for another six years while writing a dissertation."

"And a real live paycheck probably looked pretty good." Thayer tucked a wild curl off her face.

Corey swerved again to keep the truck on the road. Even in her peripheral vision, Thayer's gesture was the sexiest thing she'd ever seen. She blushed furiously when Thayer shot her a knowing glance.

"Exactly." Her gaze flicked to see Thayer's open, slightly amused expression, her eyes bright with interest.

"And your family? Are they supportive of what you do?"

"Well, it's not table talk at Thanksgiving, but I think while I floundered with indecision it kept my parents in limbo. As soon as I settled here they sold the house and retired to the Florida Keys."

"Oh, well, that's too bad."

"Yeah, I try to visit couple of times a year and do some diving."

"Ah, so that solves another mystery."

Thayer slid over in the seat and brushed her fingers down Corey's inked arm as she drove. The full sleeve extended over her shoulder and covered part of her chest with a full, vibrant underwater scene that included an elegant mermaid—head thrown back and neck arched—as the focal point surrounded by a collage of dynamic sea life.

Corey's skin sizzled at Thayer's touch and she fought a full-body shudder. "Um, yeah, it's a thing I like. Diving, I mean." She cringed inwardly at her inarticulate comment.

"And it gave you the perfect excuse to tattoo a topless woman on your arm without seeming trashy." Thayer's eyes flashed merrily.

Corey jerked the wheel again. "Uh, that's not, um, well okay, maybe." She felt Thayer's laughing eyes on her and wondered how this woman had the power to unbalance her so completely. Thayer Reynolds had her absolutely spinning, butterflies erupting in her belly every time she teased her, and Corey was both terrified and desperate for more.

She finally pulled into the lot of what looked like an old warehouse, which is exactly what it was before it was converted. "And here we are."

CHAPTER NINE

Thayer followed her in and tried unsuccessfully not to stare at her ass in her workout gear. Corey Curtis had a positively spectacular body. Well-defined shoulders and arms, perfectly sized breasts for a woman's hands, and abs, ass, and legs made of iron. Thayer's thoughts were trending toward obscene as she imagined that body underneath her and what she would do with it. Her fantasy was made all the more enticing by Corey's seeming obliviousness to how she looked to other people.

Thayer tore her eyes from Corey, ashamed her thoughts had turned so lascivious, and looked around the large open warehouse. There were several heavy bags and assorted training dummies in one corner. There was a space for fitness equipment and free weights, a large mat facing a wall of mirrors, presumably for group classes. The center of the room held a boxing ring with canvas mat and side ropes.

Thayer watched the woman in the ring, decked out in gloves and headgear as she battled an opponent wearing training pads on her hands, aiming her kicks and punches at the pads as they moved around the ring. The woman was fit and young, though smaller than Corey, with short tufts of dark hair sticking up through the headgear.

She stopped dancing around the ring when she caught sight of them. "Thought you were bailing on me, Cor."

"Yeah, sorry, Rach." She dropped her bag at the side of the ring. "I got a little held up."

Rachel's eyes trained on Thayer, widening in surprise and curiosity as she came over and leaned against the ropes. "I guess." She smiled and held out a gloved hand in Thayer's direction. "Rachel Wiley."

Thayer returned her smile and extended her arm up to grasp her hand. "Thayer Reynolds. It's very nice to meet you."

"You too." Rachel continued to stare, unashamedly. "I'm sorry, did Corey actually bring you along to watch her get her ass handed to her again?"

"Hey," Corey barked. "Be nice."

"I invited myself, actually." Thayer grinned. "I'm hoping to take her for a drink after." Her eyes flicked between Rachel and Corey. "As long as you don't hurt her too badly."

Rachel cracked up and a chorus of laughter erupted from the groups of women clustering around the ring.

"Come on, now." Corey feigned hurt and shook her head as she slipped on her gloves and climbed into the ring.

"You hoping Wiley won't give you a beatdown in front of your pretty new friend, Curtis?" someone shouted from the peanut gallery.

Corey's face flamed red and she busied herself adjusting her headgear and popping in her mouth guard.

Thayer slid onto one of the benches around the ring and tried to act like she belonged there. She was aware of the stares, some furtive and others blatant, from the other women. Usually unshakably confident, she suddenly felt very out of place. While she was no stranger to the gym, it was for Pilates, yoga, and the occasional cardio boot camp. She knew very little about mixed martial arts except that it was violent. This didn't seem like a group that usually brought a cheering section along, and she hoped she hadn't embarrassed Corey.

As easy as it would be to sit there and appreciate her body for the next half hour, Thayer took the time to examine the other things about Corey she found attractive—just about everything. She was funny, down-to-earth, and unassumingly accomplished. She seemed honest without a hint of self-righteousness. She had a powerful allure and she was drawn to her in a way she had never before experienced with another woman.

She had no idea what she was seeing as she watched the two women go at each other in a flurry of brutal kicks and punches, one of which snapped Corey's head back, viciously, sending her stumbling to one knee and bringing Thayer to her feet. She winced as Rachel stopped for a minute. She couldn't hear what they said to each other, but Rachel laughed and Corey seemed to be fine as she stood and waved at Rachel to continue.

Before they clashed again Corey's eyes flicked to her and gave her a quick smile and wave, presumably, to let her know she was all right. Thayer's heart filled at the gesture. The warmth in her chest was quickly replaced with shock and awe as they both charged the other in a tangle of limbs, battling for position. Rachel's leg swept in behind Corey and took them both down to the mat, hard. The women watching whooped and cheered as they grappled fiercely.

Thayer moved to the edge of the bench, almost unable to tell where one of them ended and the other began when Rachel locked her arms around Corey's head. She blinked and almost missed it as Corey used her longer reach to get an arm between them, locking Rachel out while she swung her hips around and hooked Rachel's neck behind her knee, breaking her hold and smoothly reversing their positions. She flipped Rachel around by the arm and locked her legs across Rachel's chest while gripping tight to her wrist and leaning back, hips thrust forward. Thayer grinned. She knew that one—an arm bar. Rachel quickly tapped out and Corey leapt to her feet, raising her arms in victory, a wide grin on her face as she roared and flexed at the women watching.

Corey helped Rachel to her feet and they laughed about something as the other women went back to their workout. Corey turned to Thayer, beaming, and raised her arms again. "Yo, Adrian, I did it!"

Thayer laughed at her endearing, unself-conscious antics. She clapped, making a concerted effort to keep her eyes on Corey's face and not rake her sweat-slicked, pumped-up body while licking her lips like a starving animal. "Good. I prefer my drinks celebratory to medicinal."

Corey laughed, her blue eyes flashing with joy and anticipation.

Thayer was so distracted she almost didn't hear her phone buzz and quickly pulled it from her pocket, recognizing the hospital number. "Dr. Reynolds." She could feel Corey's eyes on her as she pressed a finger to her other ear. She listened for a moment, her mood deflating with every word. "I'll be right there."

"What's wrong?" Corey leaned her arms across the top ropes, her brow furrowing.

She grimaced as she turned back. "There's been a multi-car accident. I'm needed back at the ED."

Corey's mouth opened and closed a couple of times. "I understand."

"I'm sorry." She felt as disappointed as Corey looked.

"No. It's your job." Corey climbed down. "I'll drive you back."

"I need to hustle." Thayer held up a hand to stop her. "I'll grab a cab." She turned and headed for the exit.

She'd only taken a few steps before she turned back to see Corey still standing, watching her. "You looked really great out there." She smiled seductively and then she was gone.

CHAPTER TEN

They walked in to Pitch Stop, a bar that while not specifically a lesbian bar, sponsored a lot of women's sports teams and had become an informal dyke hangout. It was now nicknamed by the regulars as "The Bitch." It was a classic sports bar with cheap beer on tap, fried food in baskets, loud music, and a television on every wall. They did a hilarious karaoke night once a month, collected for the local food bank, and often hired young people looking to get off the street and back on their feet. Corey approved wholeheartedly of their efforts and was friendly with Jan, the frizzy-haired, middle-aged owner, and many of the regulars. She nodded at a few of them on their way in.

"Be right back," Rachel said and headed directly to the bar while Corey slid into a booth at the back. She absently stared at a televised baseball game while she spun a cardboard coaster.

Rachel was back in minutes with a tray carrying a pitcher of beer, two shots of tequila, and a basket of cheese fries. She slid a shot to Corey and poured them each a beer. "So, let's start with this." She waited for Corey to raise her glass and they clinked them together. "Congratulations. Your win was well-deserved."

Corey threw the shot back with a grimace and reached for her beer, draining half of it. "Thank you." She eyed her friend, suspiciously. "You weren't going easy on me were you? You know because—"

"Because you showed up with the hottest, fucking woman I've ever laid eyes on?" Rachel tossed back her own drink and sucked in a breath. "I did not. But since you brought it up, where the hell did you find Dr. McSultry?"

"Cute." Corey finished her beer and refilled her glass. "First of all, you know I work at a hospital, right? Doctors also work there."

Rachel laughed. "Go on."

"Secondly, she found me." She shrugged.

"Come on, Corey, for real. What's going on? What happened with, um, Anna?" Rachel pinched a pile of fries dripping in cheese sauce and crammed them into her mouth.

"Oh, right." She winced. "Anna left me the other day. Said I was an asshole and she deserved better."

Rachel barked a laugh and raised her glass. "To a wise woman."

"Yeah, no kidding." Corey worked on another beer. "And the next day, or maybe it was the same day, Thayer Reynolds showed up in my life. And seriously, Rach, I have not known up from down since."

Rachel grinned. "She's into you."

"Weird, right?"

"Nah." Rachel spun the glass around in her hands and looked away. "It's not weird."

Corey wrinkled her brow and helped herself to the fries. "Now you're being weird."

"You have this thing. This, I don't know, calm, heroic way about you."

"Jesus, Rach. You trying to get into my pants again?"

Rachel shook her head. "It's not just me. You should hear what some of the other girls say about you in the locker room."

"Uh, hard pass."

"It's not like that. A couple of the new girls, Emily and Emma, the ones from the university, were talking the other day about being harassed pretty seriously at a party. They sounded pretty shaken about it. They both wished you'd been there. That you would've known what to do and put those cocksuckers in their place."

"Really? I mean yeah, I wouldn't have let dickheads like that treat them that way, but you know, wouldn't anyone do the same?"

"No, Corey. Not everyone would do the same. In fact, probably very few people."

"Well, I don't really know what to say." She mused on Rachel's words, and on her recent conversation with Cin. "I just do what feels right. I don't really think about it. It's just who I am."

"Well, you keep doing you, and maybe soon you'll be doing Dr. McSultry." Rachel grinned.

Corey laughed. "You are a class act."

"So, tell me about her." Rachel's eyebrows waggled.

"I admit I have completely lost my chill over this woman, which is freaking me out. We've spent a total of an hour together and that's being generous." She refilled her glass. "But I've not had enough to drink yet to share. I don't want to jinx it."

Rachel eyed her as she slid out of the booth. "Back in a sec."

It was just past midnight when the last accident victim had either been admitted or released, minus the one who had gone straight to the morgue. Thayer trudged wearily out to the staff lot making a valiant effort to remain vigilant, which is why she saw a person walking slowly between the rows and peering into windows of the twenty or so cars parked overnight.

Her eyes narrowed and she debated going back in and informing security, when the figure straightened and she recognized her immediately, her heart skipping at the sight of the broad shoulders and mussed up short hair. "Corey? What are you doing here?"

Corey jumped and whirled at her name. "Oh, shit." Her hand went to her chest. "You scared the hell out of me." Her face broke into a wide grin. "Hey."

Thayer looked her over, jeans hanging low on her hips and her faded T-shirt just brushing the top of her waistband, flashing skin when she moved just right. She swayed slightly and her eyes were bright and glassy. "Are you drunk?"

"What?" Corey held out her hands innocently. "No, I mean, no. Well, maybe a little."

She frowned. "How did you get here?" She looked around for her truck, ready to light her up if she drove.

"Rachel dropped me off."

"Okay, good. Why?"

"So, I could leave a note on your car because I didn't have your phone number," she explained.

"I see." Thayer forced down a laugh and looked around. "And how were you going to find my car?"

"Using my amazing superpowers of observation and perception about people."

Thayer laughed now. "Carry on then and I'll give you a ride home."

Thayer watched with barely contained amusement while Corey circled the cars and continued to return to the same one—a black Audi A4.

She eyed Thayer over the top of it. "This one."

Thayer arched a brow at her. "It is a nice car."

Corey looked at her expectantly. "Well?"

"Well, get in. I'll drive you home."

"I was right?" Corey's eyes flashed and she thumped her chest. "Boo-yah!" She yanked the handle of the passenger door and the alarm whooped to life, shattering the quiet of midnight. She jumped back. "Shut it off!"

"I can't." Thayer laughed and looked around wildly. "It's not my car."

Corey stared at her, stupidly.

"Come on. Come on." She grabbed Corey by the hand, pulling her across the parking lot to her ten-year-old Range Rover.

"Jesus Christ." Corey barked as she flopped into the passenger seat. "That was mean."

She was still laughing as she raced out of the parking lot before the owner of the Audi showed up. "Sorry, but I'm a big believer in what comes around goes around."

Corey shook her head and laughed. "Yeah, that was good."

Thayer grew quiet. Now that the teasing was over, something hung unspoken and heavy in the air between them. "Where do you live?"

"Not far." Corey indicated she should turn left. "I actually could have walked."

"Don't be silly. It's late."

Corey didn't speak again save for giving Thayer directions to her condo, less than two miles from the hospital. It was a quiet street of condos and bungalows.

"This is nice," she commented as she pulled up to Corey's place on the dark street.

"Yeah. It suits."

"Why did you come to the hospital tonight?" Thayer asked softly, her heart thumping hard in her chest.

"I told you."

"Hmm. Let's see it."

"What?"

"The note."

"Oh." Corey seemed to consider. "Okay." She pulled a crumpled paper from her back pocket. It was scribbled on the receipt from the bar.

Thayer took it from her and unfolded it. "Call me," she read aloud and recited Corey's phone number. "You're a woman of few words."

"But grand gestures."

"So I see." Thayer tucked the paper into her own pocket. "I will."

"Will what?"

"Call you," she replied, struggling to keep herself in her seat and not lean across and take Corey in her arms and blaze fiery kisses up and down her neck, working her way over to her lips while she slid her hands under her shirt to feel the hard muscles of her abdomen. She looked adorable and sexy and a little bewildered.

"Oh." Corey nodded. "I should go." She eased out of the car and closed the door softly behind her, leaning back in through the open window. "You must think I'm a complete lunatic."

"No." Thayer smiled and shook her head. "I don't think that of you, at all."

"What do you think?"

She offered the safest thing she could think of. "You make me laugh."

"Oh. Well, it's a start, I guess."

"Why? What do you think?"

Corey looked at her for a long time, a slow smile creeping across her face. "One day soon, Dr. Reynolds, I'd like to kiss you breathless."

She inhaled sharply, her blood heating and belly clenching. Corey's gaze smoldered over her as she gave voice to Thayer's own thoughts. "Okay," she whispered, swallowing hard.

"Okay." Corey grinned crookedly. "You have my number."

CHAPTER ELEVEN

Corey stretched, feeling the tightness in her muscles from yesterday's fight with Rachel. She rolled her head to the clock. It was barely six. Rachel wasn't picking her up for another hour to take her to the gym and pick up her truck. She should definitely make time for a light workout, too, to ease some of the stiffness and sweat out her hangover. She smacked her lips and tried to work up a swallow around her pasty mouth. She needed to be far more careful. Two women-induced binges was getting the week off to a rocky start.

She stared at the ceiling as the memories of last night came flooding back. She groaned a laugh, vacillating between being impressed with herself and thoroughly disgusted. Thayer sought her out, waited for her, and wanted to buy her a drink. When she had other plans, Thayer wanted to come with. That was not nothing. Corey had somehow managed to beat Rachel for the first time while she was watching. That pleased her. Her level of disappointment that Thayer got called back to work seemed out of proportion with how long they had known each other.

She had a good time with Rachel. They hadn't been out in a while and Rachel was relentless at keeping Corey real. It was good to talk to her about the end of her relationship with Anna and the beginning of one with Thayer. She covered her face and sighed. Then to cap off the night, she drunk stalked Thayer's car, set off a stranger's car alarm and was, in general, a complete idiot.

The look on Thayer's face when Corey told her she wanted to kiss her breathless may have been the one thing that made the entire fiasco worth it. She tried to convince herself it was just the alcohol talking, and she'd let her mouth run away from her, but she knew however she tried to spin it, she meant it with every fiber of her being. She had rarely said anything like that to someone she was dating and certainly never to someone she had just met. But it rolled easily off her tongue and it had stunned the totally composed Thayer Reynolds.

The Pandora's box of Corey's libidinous thoughts was opened at the memory of Thayer's parted lips and gorgeous golden eyes, wide with surprise and mutual desire. She was extraordinary and Corey closed her eyes, inviting the fantasy to consume her. She could imagine Thayer stretched out beneath her, taut and trembling at her touch, full breasts and pointed nipples arching against her hands, hips thrusting against her.

Corey groaned as the damp ache between her legs grew urgent, and she slid her own hand down to feel her slick arousal. The image flipped in her mind as she stroked herself, imagining Thayer straddling her, grinding down on her hand with her back arched and head thrown back in ecstasy while Corey buried her fingers inside her, their hips rolling in concert.

She clenched around her own desperate fingers as she came hard and fast with Thayer on her mind. "Oh, God." She breathed heavily, turning into her pillow. "What the fuck am I doing?"

Corey badged herself in through the loading dock. She was so lost in thought about what was happening to her and wondering if she was losing her mind that she walked directly into Jim Collier.

He jumped to avoid her, his hands jerking and sloshing hot coffee over his shirt front. "Jesus, Curtis! Watch where you're going."

"Damn," she said, wincing. "I totally didn't see you, Collier." She brushed ineffectually at his clothes.

"No shit." He frowned at her and backed away. "One of these was for you but I've changed my mind."

She pouted as she opened the morgue door. "Oh, don't be like that."

He followed her in and set the cups on the desk and wiped at his tie. "Christ." He glared at her. "What's got you all dopey faced?"

She straightened her expression. "What do you mean?"

"Don't even bother." He handed her a cup. "I already know." He pulled a folded square of paper from his shirt pocket. It was slightly damp with coffee. "Serves you right if you can't read it now."

She took the paper and carefully teased it open to avoid tearing it. Her heart leapt when she saw it was a prescription page from Dr. Thayer Reynolds. The written message was hastily scrawled, but her script was smooth and classic. The message sent Corey's pulse through the roof. *Dinner tonight. 8:00 p.m. Pick me up in the ED.*

She folded it and tucked it in her pocket. "What?"

He was staring at her. "If I could bottle your face right now, I would be a wealthy man."

She shrugged, unable to deny how giddy the invitation had just made her. "She gave the note to you? Did you read it?"

"Yeah and no. I don't give a shit about your love life, Curtis." He dug in a pocket for his notebook. "My night shift officers took garbage statements from the victims of the car crash so I had to follow up on a few things in the ED earlier. Plus, you got one down here I need to see about."

Corey couldn't help a grin. Thayer could have called but decided to play along with Corey's ridiculous note writing. "Thanks," she said dreamily.

He snapped his fingers in front of her face. "Can we get to work now?"

"Yes. Sorry." She took a big gulp of her coffee and flipped open the file left on her desk from the police when they brought him in. "This your guy?"

He peered over her shoulder. "Yep." He referred to his notes. "Dead on scene. The family has requested an external only and Doc Webster has agreed."

"Good on him."

She wasn't sorry she didn't have to do another full post on a tragically mangled person. It wasn't unusual in the case of an instant or near instant death in some obviously accidental manner for the family to request an external exam only to spare their loved one any further perceived indignity.

"Sure." He was taking notes from the information in the file. Information he had access to six other ways, but as far as he was concerned, if it wasn't in his book it didn't happen.

"Speaking of dead bodies…" she called from inside the cooler. She wheeled a gurney out loaded with a heavy-duty, black vinyl body bag.

"Were we?"

"Yes." She maneuvered the gurney up against the autopsy table and lined it up to transfer the body. "And not this one, by the way," she gritted out as she moved the body across still inside the bag. She was hoping she could get away without moving him. "Did you get my report on Gordon Akers?"

"Who?"

"The fall at the construction site?" She unzipped the bag to reveal her guy was in fact a girl—a young one. "Damn," she breathed as she looked at the ruined body, deformed limbs and skull split open.

"Masters, MacKenzie, twenty-year-old, white female, in her third year at the university." He came over and looked at the body. His eye was twitching like it did when he got very angry. "My youngest just turned twenty."

"Sorry," she mumbled, unsure how to respond. The tragic death of young people was always so affecting, not matter how hardened you grew.

"For what?" He cleared his throat erasing any trace of emotion. "That ain't her." He stepped away from the table. "And yes, I got your report. Your attention to detail never fails to amaze. What was that? Like twenty pages?"

"Thirteen," she replied, waiting as he took his notes. "And?"

"And what, Curtis? You want a pat on the back for doing your job? Go ask your boss."

Collier was in a mood today and she debated just dropping it, but she couldn't let it go. "I want to know what you think of the depressed skull fracture on his posterior skull. I would like you to consider it a signature fracture and that there may have been something other than the fall that caused it."

He snapped his book closed and took his time tucking it back into his pocket before he responded. "Like what?"

"I don't know. It's a construction site—a brick, a block, a beam, a board?" As soon as the words were out of her mouth she grimaced, waiting for it.

"Or some other alliterative object?" he asked, dryly. "Don't quit your day job, Curtis."

"This is my goddamn day job, Collier."

He sighed. "What did Webster say?"

Corey thinned her lips. "He hasn't replied to my report."

"Well, when he does, and if he has concerns about the cause or manner of death, then we'll take another look at it."

"Fine," she said through clenched teeth as she turned to the body in front of her. "In the meantime I'll get this one out to you by the end of the day. I'll try to keep it short."

He studied her a moment before he turned to leave. "Good luck on your date," he called as the door closed.

Her head snapped up from behind the camera. "Bastard." She grumbled but she didn't really mean it. Collier was the kind of friend who would never say it out loud, but if she ever needed anything, he would be there. And he most definitely was interested in her love life. That had always been obvious.

CHAPTER TWELVE

Cin showed up five minutes after Collier left and was all too happy to take the lead on the crash victim, after she spent some time contemplating her own mortality and wondering if the young woman was someone she ever passed on campus, saw lounging on the quad, or bumped into at the coffee cart.

Blessedly she was not one of Cin's students, but when word got around of her death, Cin would keep an ear out for people who knew her, assuring them her death was swift and likely painless and she was well taken care of afterward.

Now, though, like everyone in the death industry, medical or otherwise, she shut it all down and became the scientist she was. She took photos, measured and described injuries in precise, clinical detail while Corey supervised and took notes.

When they were through, Dr. Webster ambled down, took a look, and approved and signed the death certificate—catastrophic trauma to the head and torso.

Cin packed the body away and cleaned up while Corey wrote and proofread the brief report and sent it off to Dr. Webster and Collier.

Corey was done by three and spent the rest of the afternoon mindlessly clicking through her mandatory safety training modules, trying hard not to worry about what she was going to wear to dinner. At five she headed home.

She stood in the shower for a long time, contemplating the loaded gun theory and wondering when she became so randy. The sheets hadn't even been changed since the last time she and Anna were together. It wasn't like she was just coming off a months' long dry spell. There was just something so sensual about Thayer that turned her on so hard and so fast it left her head spinning.

She had plenty of time still, so she threw on a robe, changed the sheets and made the bed while still damp from the shower. She threw in a load of laundry, did the dishes, bagged up the trash and wiped down the counters.

She was far from a slob, but with no one to impress she tended to back burner a lot. She couldn't even remember if she had ever cleaned up for Anna. Likely it was Anna who had cleaned and she just never noticed.

She leaned against the bathroom sink and studied herself in the mirror, trying to avoid getting down on herself for being such a jerk. Anna was right; this was going to haunt her and she was starting to have second thoughts about going out with Thayer. Maybe she just wasn't relationship material.

In a fit of low self-esteem, she decided to call Thayer and cancel but two problems presented themselves immediately. She still didn't know Thayer's number and she seemed to have left her phone in the morgue, probably on her desk.

"Damn it." She flopped onto the couch with a beer. It was only quarter to seven. She sucked on her beer and eyed her tidy place, wondering exactly what made her think Thayer would be coming home with her tonight. "Your looks and charm, of course."

She debated the wisdom of it while drinking a second beer and stood in front of her closet. Why was this so hard? Thayer had already seen her in her rattiest clothes, scrubs, and her workout gear. Why was this different?

Unable to come to a satisfactory answer, or at least one she was willing to admit to herself, she slipped into jeans—faded but not ripped, and the ones she had been told made her ass look great. She slid a wide black leather belt through the loops and pulled her soft white button-down from the hanger. It was clean and had even been pressed, probably by Anna.

She gelled her hair lightly, brushed her teeth, and unable to recall if she had brushed up against deodorant she reapplied. Her black eye was barely noticeable and she didn't have makeup to cover it with had she wanted to.

She slid her feet into black leather low-heeled boots and decided she had enough time to run back to the morgue and get her phone.

She glanced around the empty loading dock as she pulled in. All delivery trucks and maintenance vehicles were long gone for the day and there were no more porters smoking in the corner near the overflowing ashtray. The only movement now was loose trash blowing around the overstuffed Dumpster. It was just starting to get dark, the sun lowering and elongating the shadows, but she could still make out the closed bay doors, stacked shipping pallets, and darkened windows at this hour.

She waved her badge over the sensor at the back door, flipping it over when the light stubbornly stayed red and then smearing it violently against the sensor pad, first one direction and then the other. "Come on, you bastard," she growled. It beeped finally and turned green. She jerked the door open just as she heard heavy, fast steps behind her and a rustle of movement. She turned and something heavy and hard slammed into the back of her head. She staggered forward with a shout of pain and dropped to the cement floor just inside the door.

She tried to get up. She could feel the stream of warm, thick blood cascading from the back of her head onto the floor. "Shit."

She got one arm under her only to have it jerked painfully away from her body as someone dragged her through the door and into the morgue by the wrist. He was strong, and despite the ever-present smell of death and chemicals, she could smell booze and body odor.

She craned to see him but her vision blurred and something covered his face. The pain in her head was piercing as he released her. She groaned as she struggled to get her arms beneath her again.

"Stay down," he barked from somewhere close by.

She heard the crash of steel onto the floor and the slamming of cabinets. Her vision grayed in and out, wavering sickeningly. She swallowed heavily, closing her eyes against the nausea, pain, and disorientation and stayed still, unable to process what was happening and what she should be doing about it.

"Where is it?" the voice howled. "Fuck."

There was a dull thump followed by the gurgle of liquid splashing onto the floor. Her head jerked toward the sound, sending streaking pain through the back of her skull and her stomach roiled at the movement.

"No." She gasped as he overturned the recently opened five-gallon cube of formalin and poured its contents onto the floor.

The acrid fumes hit her immediately, her eyes tearing and a gagging cough ripping from her throat as the toxic chemicals pooled around her, seeping into her clothes on her left side. She needed to get up—now.

"Goddamn it," he choked, splashing through the puddle as he ran out the back door.

Thayer put the finishing touches on her makeup in the doctor's lounge. Corey may already be waiting for her. She hadn't meant to be fashionably late, a trait she found obnoxious and unnecessary. She thought she had left herself enough time to clean up and get changed, but as usual, someone came along and held her up.

She planned to ask Corey out to dinner this morning. Initially she had intended to text the invitation, but when she saw Jim Collier in the ED scribbling away in his notebook, she had a flash of brilliance. She knew Corey would appreciate the humor in a handwritten note. She realized later she had no way of knowing whether or not the invitation had been received or accepted and Corey still didn't have her number. She could text to confirm, but that would take the fun out of it and she was all but certain Corey would be there.

What she hadn't thought about was where they were going to go, and now she was concerned she was overdressed. She smoothed her hands down her sapphire blue silk blouse and black, wide-legged pants. She had removed the clip from her hair and let her curls fall loosely down her back. Her heels clicked across the linoleum as she walked back out to the admitting station, paying no attention to the heads turning as she went.

"Holy shit, Thayer." Dana eyed her up and down. "Are you trying to kill her?"

"That comes later." Thayer winked.

Dana continued to stare along with half the department. "Tell me again why we never…" She trailed off and waggled her eyebrows.

Thayer laughed. "Um, because you're like a negative on the Kinsey scale."

"Right. I don't even want to look at my own boobs sometimes. But good lord, Thayer, if it was going to be anyone, it would be you."

"Well." Thayer beamed at her. "Thank you for that. I'm holding out for someone else tonight, however." She checked her watch with a frown. It was well after eight.

"Don't worry," Dana assured her as she grabbed a stack of charts and headed off. "She'll be here."

"I'm just going to run and check downstairs. Maybe she got held up."

Dana waved and disappeared down the hall. "Have a great time."

Corey groaned and coughed as she struggled to her feet, staggering and going down to one knee before she could push herself up using the autopsy table. She raised a shaky hand to the back of her head feeling a thick swelling and a lot of blood dripping down her neck and back, soaking her shirt.

She stumbled to the formalin box and righted it with effort, streaming tears and wheezing between coughs as the harsh fumes filled the room. She couldn't see the box's cap so she grabbed a towel from the counter and stuffed it through the opening.

She looked around, disoriented, at the instruments and supplies pulled out of every drawer and cabinet. They skittered across the floor with a clang of metal as she staggered toward the two big plastic containers of aldehyde neutralizing agent. It took her several tries to fumble the lids off, her hands trembling and slippery with blood. She could barely see as she dumped the granules all over the floor where the formalin had pooled, absorbing and solidifying the liquid.

She was starting to feel the burn against her skin, her drenched shirt plastered to her left side and arm with the corrosive chemical. She knew she was going to be in trouble if she didn't get out of her clothes.

Thayer smelled the pungent chemical as soon as she came through the stairwell, the back of her hand going to her nose as she gave a sharp cough. "What the hell?" She looked down and saw smears of fresh blood across the floor from the outside door and her heart ratcheted up a notch.

She pushed open the door to the morgue and the odor was overwhelming, her eyes immediately burning and tearing. "Corey!"

"Stay back," she choked and Thayer heard her labored breathing. "Don't come in."

"Like hell." Corey leaned heavily against the autopsy table, fumbling with the buttons on her blood-soaked, white shirt.

Thayer's heart went to her throat for a moment before her training took over. She moved in front of her, ripping her soaked shirt open and jerking it off her shoulders, leaving her only in her bra. Her skin was blotchy and red on the left side. "Look at me," she demanded, hooking a finger beneath Corey's chin and guiding her head up gently.

Corey's head wobbled on blood-streaked shoulders and she could barely open her red, swollen eyes.

"Jesus. Did you ingest any of it?"

"No," Corey croaked. "There was someone here. We need to call the police."

"You first."

Thayer wanted to get her right to the ED, treat her eyes and breathing and find out where that blood was coming from, but she would contaminate everything. She spied the emergency shower. "Over here." She helped her up and over to the shower. She kept one arm around Corey's waist and pulled the chain handle with the other.

The water was bitterly cold as it rained over them both and Corey shivered. "I know it's cold. Turn your face into it. We need to wash out your eyes."

Corey did as instructed as Thayer pumped liquid soap into her hands from the dispenser on the wall and smeared it all over Corey's left side and arm. She could now see the blood streaming from the back of her head and she could just make out the edges of a ragged wound through her short hair. "Oh, honey, who did this to you?"

Corey's breathing became more irregular and her coughing near constant as she shivered under the water. Thayer shut it off and snatched a lab coat from the wall hook. "Time to go." Though the absorbent material had done its job, it was too dangerous to stay longer. She threw the coat over Corey's shoulders and grabbed a clean green towel from the counter, folding it and pressing it to the back of Corey's head.

Corey groaned at the pressure, her steps faltering.

"I know. I'm sorry." Thayer kept a tight grip on her waist. "You have to help me. You're bleeding a lot. Hold this here."

Corey's hand jerked up to hold the towel against the back of her head as they made their way out of the morgue.

CHAPTER THIRTEEN

"Dana, I need you." Thayer moved as fast as possible through the department. "Is there a curtain free?"

Dana's eyes widened in shock. "Uh, six, all the way at the end."

Dana came around to Corey's other side and guided her. "God, what is that smell? What the hell happened?"

Thayer shook her head as they eased Corey onto the gurney and closed the curtain. "I'm not sure. Acute formalin exposure, inhaled and absorbed, head lac, possible concussion and skull fracture. Breathing is labored, chemical burns on her left flank and arm."

"I got it." Dana was cutting off the rest of Corey's clothes and covering her with a sheet. "Send Jules in and get changed."

"Check her pressure, and O2 sats, start an IV with normal saline, saline rinse for her eyes, supplemental oxygen and call CT—"

"I got it, Thayer." Dana looked at her sharply. "Get changed and then you can come back and boss me around."

It took Thayer mere minutes to strip out of her clothes, throw on scrubs and tie her hair back. By the time she got back, Corey was breathing beneath an oxygen mask. The finger of her right hand was tipped with the pulse oximeter, a blood pressure cuff was wrapped around her upper arm, and an IV was running into the back of her hand. Her head was swathed in a fresh gauze bandage.

Jules was standing by her head flushing her eyes with a bottle of saline and Dana was smearing topical antibiotic and analgesic along her arm and side.

Thayer hit the button on the automated blood pressure monitor, inflating the cuff. She waited impatiently as the monitor cycled through before flashing the reading 97/60. "What was it before?"

"It was 85 over 50," Dana answered.

"Okay, it's heading in the right direction." Thayer slid the stethoscope from around her neck, inserting the ear tips and placing the diaphragm on Corey's chest beneath the sheet. "Corey, how are you feeling?"

"Bet...better," she rasped from behind the mask.

"Good." Thayer moved the diaphragm across her chest. "Deep breath."

Corey inhaled, shakily, eliciting a painful-sounding cough with the effort.

Thayer moved her hand to the other side. "Again." The result was the same. "One more time. Any pain with breathing?" Thayer listened for a while longer then moved the stethoscope back around her neck.

"Chest is tight," Corey managed around another cough.

"I'll bet." Thayer smiled at her. "There's no fluid in your lungs but your airways are inflamed and constricted, which is why it's hard to breathe. It will improve quickly and clear up entirely in a day or two."

Corey nodded and winced at the movement.

"I'm going to check out your head now." She motioned for Jules to stop the saline rinse, grabbed a towel and gently wiped Corey's face. "How's her O2?"

Dana glanced at the monitor. "Ninety-eight percent."

"Okay, we can take this off." Thayer gently removed the oxygen mask. "Did you call CT?"

"They're ready whenever we are."

"Thanks." She turned her attention back to her patient as she gently palpated the back of her head. "How are you doing, Corey?" She pulled out her penlight, gently lifting her lids and shining it in each eye in turn. "Pupils are equal and reactive."

"Tired," came the raspy reply as her red, irritated eyes blinked sluggishly.

"I know, honey. It's probably just the adrenaline crash, but you have to stay awake, okay? The neurologist is going to want to talk to you and assess for concussion." Thayer checked her neck with firm, gentle fingers. "How's the pain? Scale of one to ten."

Corey attempted a smile. "Two."

"Liar." Thayer smiled. "Can you tell me what day it is?"

"Our first date day." Corey wheezed and coughed violently enough for Thayer to reach for the oxygen again, while she smoothed damp hair from her face.

"I'm afraid we're going to have to take a rain check on that." She smiled around the tightness in her throat. "Just breathe easy, honey."

"Didn't even get to see what you were wearing," Corey whispered.

Dana gave her arm a gentle a squeeze. "If you weren't already here, you'd have probably had a heart attack."

Corey rolled her eyes to her and smiled. "I believe you."

"No fractures that I can feel, but CT is going to take a look and make sure you don't have a bleed or any swelling." She nodded to Jules, who released the brakes on the gurney with her foot and pushed from the head. "I'll be here when you're done."

Corey reached her arm out to brush Thayer's hand. "Thank you."

Thayer took a deep shuddering breath, her hand going to her chest as Corey was wheeled away.

Dana placed a hand on her arm. "You okay?"

"Yeah." Thayer breathed deeply. "Yes. I will be." She offered a small smile. "Thanks for your help."

"She won't be back for a while. You want a cup of coffee?"

"Yeah, thanks." Thayer pulled out her cell from her back pocket and dropped onto a stool. "I need to make a phone call."

Thayer straightened from her slouch against the counter when she heard the familiar rattle of gurney wheels down the hallway. Corey was looking pale and exhausted by the time she returned an hour later, her gurney steered in by a porter. Her eyes were red-rimmed and bloodshot but open. At some point she had been helped into a set of scrubs, and there was a thick bandage around her head, blood already seeping through. Her IV had been removed.

"Hey, tough girl." Thayer smiled, gently. "How did it go?" She picked up the report from atop the sheet across her legs.

"Super fun times." Corey winced as she shifted on the bed.

"Everything looks clear." Thayer sighed in relief and tossed the pages onto the counter. CT and the neurologist had already called but it was good to see it in writing. No swelling or hemorrhaging and no conclusive indicators of concussion. "I called plastics. They're going to come see about getting you stitched up but it may be a while."

"Plastic surgery? I don't want those butchers touching me. You can do it."

"Oh, Corey." Thayer shook her head. "I'm glad you haven't lost your sense of humor but they'll do a much better job."

"It's the back of my head, and anyway don't chicks dig scars?"

"Not the ones they're responsible for."

Corey frowned. "You're not responsible for this, Thayer. Now come on. My head is killing me and I need to call the police. Plus, it hurts to talk so I can't argue with you."

Thayer pursed her lips before she set up a sterile tray. "I already did. Jim is downstairs with a couple of officers checking out the morgue, and environmental services is standing by to clean up when he gives the all clear. He should be up to talk to you shortly."

Jules slipped in through the curtain. "Hey, I heard you were back." She moved over next to Corey and placed a hand on her leg. "Are you okay? Can I get you anything?"

"I'm okay, thanks, Jules." Corey managed a smile for her.

Jules patted her leg. "Let me know if you need anything."

Thayer waved Jules out and turned to arch an amused brow in Corey's direction. "You two seemed to have turned a corner."

"Yeah, well, I gave her a bottle of wine and she's seen me naked."

"Is that so?" Thayer moved the tray over next to the bed. "I guess your relationship has gone to the next level."

Corey breathed a laugh. "You got to rip my shirt off."

Thayer pulled a stool over and sat down. "Yes, well, that wasn't really the scenario in which I had imagined that happening."

Corey blinked at her. "Oh, really?"

Thayer felt her face flush but was saved from answering.

"Everyone decent?" Collier announced himself before pulling the curtain aside. "Holy Mary, mother of God. Curtis, you look like shit."

"Yeah, being brained with a pipe will do that."

"A brick," he corrected. "We found it by the loading dock door. Feel up to telling me what happened?"

"Yeah, okay." Corey's eyes flicked to Thayer. "Can you work while we talk?"

"I'm good." Thayer loaded a syringe with lidocaine. "This is just a local. I'm going to hit you with something stronger after you give your statement. Then I'll take you home." Thayer encouraged her to roll onto her right side and unwrapped the bandage. "You're not squeamish are you, Jim?"

Collier barked a laugh. "Please, I've been a cop for twenty-five years and I was married with two kids."

Thayer pushed a few drops of fluid through the tip of the syringe. "This is going to hurt, Corey. Last chance to wait for plastics."

She gritted her teeth. "Just do it." She clutched the edge of the gurney. "Please."

Thayer injected anesthetic into three different spots in the angry, tender tissue around the wound. She felt Corey tense beneath her gloved hands and heard her hiss a breath. "Okay, all done. We'll just give that a minute." She rubbed Corey's shoulder. "You doing okay?"

"Yep," Corey grunted.

Thayer uncapped a sterile razor and gently shaved around the wound. It wasn't long, two inches at most but it was deep and jagged and head wounds bleed a lot. "I'm going to start with some subcutaneous sutures. They'll dissolve on their own." She flushed the wound with saline. "Ready?"

"Go." Corey tensed as Thayer reapproximated the edges of the wound with her left hand and got to work suturing. "Not so bad." Corey exhaled. "Go ahead, Collier, hit me. Figuratively speaking."

"Just tell me what happened and we can go from there."

"Um, I left my phone on my desk, and as I was badging myself in from the outside door, I heard movement behind me. I turned, got hit from behind and went down. I tried to get up but he grabbed my arm and dragged me into the morgue. Nothing seemed to work right and my vision was all messed up."

Thayer's hands stilled and she sucked in a sharp breath. "Jesus."

"You're not messing up my head back there, are you?"

Thayer refocused. "Don't you worry about me. The back of your head was the first thing about you I noticed. I'll take good care of it."

Collier snorted a laugh. "Did you see him?"

"No. He may have been wearing something over his face. A bandana maybe. I looked at him, I think, but I didn't see his face." Her voice grew tense. "I felt really sick and I tried to move but I couldn't make anything work."

"Did he say anything?"

"Yeah, um…" Corey paused. "He said, 'Stay down.' And then later, 'Where is it?' or something like that."

"Yeah, well, it's pretty clear he was looking for something. Any idea what?"

"No." Corey's voice sounded fatigued. "No, I don't have anything."

"You don't keep drugs or anything in there?"

"My patients are way past treatment."

"All right. We'll work on that." He jotted a quick note in his book. "Then he just left?"

Corey shook her head.

"No, honey, don't move." Thayer stilled her with a hand to her back.

"Sorry." Corey took a breath. "I think he would have stayed longer but he dumped the formalin. Didn't know what it was. It was everywhere and pooling around me. He started coughing. We both did. Then he took off. I knew I needed to get up. I stopped the spill and threw down both spill kits. That's when Thayer found me."

"Yeah, the doc already filled me on that. Anything else you can think of?"

"He smelled bad."

"Bad how?"

"Like booze and BO and stale smoke."

Collier scribbled some more. "That's good, Curtis."

There were a couple snips of scissors in the quiet that followed. "I'm all done," Thayer said softly as she bandaged the neatly closed wound. "Do you have everything you need from her?"

"For now, yeah." He snapped his notebook closed. "I don't want you going home, Curtis. This is probably random but if this asshole thinks you have something he wants, he could come looking for you again. You have somewhere you can go?"

"Um, maybe Rachel's, I guess. Or I can call Cin." Her voice was fading.

"I'll take her home with me," Thayer said, casually as she loaded a fresh syringe.

"You will?" Corey and Jim blurted at the same time.

"Yes, I will." Thayer eased Corey's scrub pants down and swiped her hip with an alcohol swab. "Hold still." She stuck her fast, injecting the contents.

"Jesus, Thayer," Corey yelped. "Buy a girl a drink first. Oh, shit, what did you do to me?" She sighed, her voice growing thick and slow.

Thayer pulled her pants back up and patted her thigh. "Shot you full of Demerol."

"Whoa." Corey rolled gracelessly onto her back, her head lolling drunkenly to the side.

"Best first date ever, huh, Curtis?" Collier asked.

Her eyes rolled toward him but couldn't maintain contact. She smiled, sloppily. "Yeah."

Thayer poked her head out of the curtain. "Jules, can you bring us a wheelchair and the kit I packed?"

Jules showed up within a minute and helped load their nearly insensible patient into the chair. "Take care, Corey." She bent to kiss her cheek.

"Bye, Jules." Corey grinned, crookedly. "You are very cute."

Collier laughed out loud.

"Come on, tough girl." Thayer pushed her toward the door.

"We're going to your place?" Corey tried to drop her head back to look at her. "But I have clean sheets."

CHAPTER FOURTEEN

Corey was dragged from her unnaturally heavy sleep by the maddening prickling sensation of the skin on her left side and the urgent need to pee. She blinked slowly as the room swam into view. She was in a large, four-poster bed with intricate scrollwork, under soft, worn sheets and an old floral quilt. There were matching bedside tables and a dresser with a mirror on the wall opposite the bed. Not at all how she would have imagined Thayer's house.

Thayer's house. She remembered that much with hazy, dreamlike memories of a soft voice and gentle touch against her cheek, encouraging her to open her eyes several times overnight.

She sat up with a groan, her stomach turning over as her head pounded and vision swirled for a moment before clearing. The room was dim but a light to her right let her know she didn't have to go far for the bathroom. She lurched to her feet, swaying slightly, as she made her way over.

She read the note Thayer had left on the sink, instructing her to help herself to whatever she needed, not to get her sutures wet, and if she was not already back from her errands, she would be shortly. She left her cell number and told Corey where she could find her phone, recovered from the morgue last night.

Corey leaned against the sink, noticing the new toothbrush, bar of soap, and toothpaste arranged on top of a fresh towel, loose cotton pants, and a T-shirt she assumed was Thayer's.

She plucked at her scrubs, feeling like she still smelled of formalin and thinking a long hot shower would relieve the discomfort on her skin. She pulled her scrub top off carefully and stripped out of her pants.

Thayer was sitting on the bed waiting for her when she emerged half an hour later, steam billowing out behind her, as she gently ran a towel over her head. "Hi," Corey rasped, her voice still gravelly.

"Feel better?" Thayer smiled at her.

"Much. I think I could—" Corey froze, her expression clouding before a painful cough rattled from her chest. Her hand went to her chest, her eyes going wide, feeling like iron bands had tightened around her.

"Whoa. Whoa." Thayer was up like a shot, gripping her around the waist and guiding her to sit on the bed.

"I...can't...bre..." Corey gasped, her panic intensifying the tightness in her chest.

"Easy. Easy." Thayer jerked up a bag that was on the floor, ripping out an albuterol inhaler from its box. "Just relax. I got you." She shook the inhaler, popped the cap off and held it to Corey's lips, her hand on the back of her neck. "Deep breath. Deep as you can." She depressed the medication as Corey's mouth closed around it and she wheezed. "Again."

Corey's eyes rolled wildly as she continued to struggle, her vision graying out, her arms dropping to her sides.

"It's okay. Don't be afraid. The meds will work." Thayer guided her back against the pillows, lifting her legs to the bed as her breathing slowly began to deepen and even out.

Corey's eyes drifted closed as she concentrated on her breathing, trying to stay calm as she felt the tightness in her chest loosen. She coughed again and took her first full breath in what felt like hours. "Okay," she whispered. "I'm okay."

Thayer exhaled. "That was kind of scary, huh?"

"What the hell was that?" she croaked, opening her eyes.

Thayer set the inhaler on the bedside table. "Your lungs are temporarily damaged from the formalin. You'll be okay, but at least for a while, you're going to be pretty sensitive. I think the steam from your shower triggered a bronchospasm. Pretty much an asthma attack."

"Shit." Corey sighed and rubbed a hand over her chest. "I feel like I just ran a marathon while smoking a pack of cigarettes."

Thayer laughed. "Feel like letting me check you out?"

Her eyes widened, her mouth quirking in amusement.

"Your head," Thayer corrected. "And your body. Your health. Shut up before you asphyxiate."

Corey wheezed a laugh. "Whose room is this?"

Thayer checked her pulse and took her blood pressure. "My grandmother's," she answered absently as she stared at her watch.

"Jesus." Corey sat up with a start and hissed a breath, the movement making her head pound. "Is she here? Where is she?"

"What?" Thayer steadied her with a hand on her shoulder. "No. She's not here anymore."

"Oh." Corey cringed. "I'm really sorry."

"No." Thayer shook her head. "She's not dead. Will you just lie still and let me do this, please?" She held up her stethoscope.

Corey relaxed back against the pillows, her smile sheepish. "Sorry."

Thayer popped in the ear tips and slipped her hand beneath the neck of Corey's T-shirt, listening to her heart and lungs.

Corey's heart rate leapt when Thayer's fingers brushed across the top of her breast and she felt the heat rise in her face. Thayer raised a brow, her gaze flicking to her briefly. "Should I check your blood pressure again?"

"Shit," Corey mumbled, knowing Thayer could hear the pounding in her chest.

Thayer's face remained unreadable. "Sit up for a second." She helped her lean forward. "I want to look at your head."

Corey sat forward and turned her head, feeling Thayer's fingers gently prodding the wound.

"Looks good. Sutures are staying put and no sign of infection." Thayer encouraged her to recline again as she took out her penlight and checked her eyes. "Headache? Blurred vision? Nausea?"

"Yes, no, and sometimes."

"Hmm." Thayer regarded her carefully.

"What's the prognosis?" Corey asked when she was quiet a long time.

"You're going to be fine," Thayer answered finally. "It may take a few days, though, so don't push yourself. Carry the inhaler, drink lots of water, no exercise for a few days or really anything that's going to elevate your breathing or heart rate and absolutely no MMA anything for a while."

Corey absently rubbed her right hand up and down her left arm to try and lessen the prickling sensation.

Thayer frowned at her arm. "Is your skin burning?"

She dropped her hand. "It's just this uncomfortable prickling feeling."

Thayer reached back in the bag for a tube of topical analgesic. "This will help." She squeezed off a generous amount into her palm and motioned for Corey to extend her arm.

Corey hesitated, briefly, searching Thayer's eyes for some indication of her intentions, immediate and otherwise.

Thayer seemed to read her unease correctly. "It's okay." She nodded and smiled gently. "I'm a doctor."

She leaned forward, extending her arm, trying to breathe evenly while Thayer smoothed the cream into her skin, gently running her hands from her shoulder to her wrist.

"Is this okay?" Thayer's voice was smokier than usual as her fingers trailed across her neck and collarbone.

Corey's heart thundered in her chest at the touch, thankful Thayer wasn't listening now with her stethoscope. Her breath quickened as she met Thayer's gaze. "I thought this was against the rules."

Thayer jerked her hands away, clearly embarrassed that her treatment had so obviously turned into something else entirely. "I'm sorry."

She sat back, a slow smile on her lips, thankful it wasn't her embarrassment this time. "What now?"

Thayer shrugged. "I could tell you about my grandmother?"

Corey's eyes widened. "Is that like a conversational cold shower?"

"Do you need one?" Thayer laughed.

Thayer led Corey out of the bedroom, down a short hall, past another bedroom she assumed was Thayer's, a second full bath, and into the most spectacular great room and farm-style kitchen she had ever seen. The floors were polished hardwood, the high ceilings exposed post and beam, and in the center sat a two-sided stone chimney rising up through the ceiling with well-loved, overstuffed sectional sofas facing the fireplace. "Wow."

Thayer moved behind the large granite island. "When's the last time you ate?" She opened the refrigerator and ducked in. "I ran to the store this morning and picked up some groceries."

"Um, yesterday afternoon, maybe," Corey answered as she walked to a wall of sliding glass doors that opened onto a large wraparound deck. One section was screened in and furnished with sun-faded, wicker lounges and the other open to the morning sunshine. There were several weather-beaten Adirondack chairs, wooden side tables and a large, shiny propane grill. Steps from the deck led down to the rocky yard, gardens, and the most gorgeous shimmering lake.

"Where are we?" Corey asked, trying to remember the drive last night.

"Beautiful, isn't it?" Thayer came to stand next to her and handed her a cup of coffee. "Black."

"Thank you." Corey smiled, their fingers brushing together as she met her eyes. "Stunning," she answered quietly.

Thayer held her gaze for a moment before turning to look out. A small dock jutted out and there was a small outboard boat tied up. A canoe rested on its side near the waterline. "We're only about ten miles outside the city, down Old South Road."

Corey considered a moment. "This is Rankins Lake?" She looked around in wonder. "I had no idea there were houses out here." She was somewhat familiar with the area. There were a few private swimming spots popular with college kids, some decent hiking and mountain biking trails around the lake, and decent bass fishing.

"There aren't very many houses." Thayer handed Corey binoculars from a nearby table and pointed across the lake. "You can just make out the white of a fishing cabin directly across from me. See their dock in front of the small clearing? Well, it's a trailer they plunked down on the property but that's what they use it for, I think. They bring up a pretty nice boat, anyway. That's my nearest neighbor." She moved back toward the kitchen and talked over her shoulder while Corey surveyed the lake. "Nana bought this land forty years ago for a song after she and my grandfather divorced. You can't buy private property out here now and you certainly can't have a house this close to the water with all the rezoning they've done. She was forty, only ten years older than I am now, but the kids were already off and doing their own thing. I still have a hard time wrapping my head around that. The house was here but I daresay it did not look like this when she took over. She's put a lot of work into it over her lifetime."

"It's amazing." Corey set the binoculars aside and looked back over the interior. "She did the work herself?"

"Some of it. I helped in the summer but the bulk of it was contracted." Thayer clattered a pan onto the gas stove. "You eat meat, right?"

"Yes." Corey's hand hovered over the door handle as she looked back at Thayer. "May I?"

Thayer glanced at her. "Please. I'll join you in a few minutes."

Thayer watched Corey step out onto the deck, barefoot, hair tousled, wearing nothing but her own lounge pants and T-shirt, which fit her surprisingly well considering how differently they were built.

Her smile faltered when she hunched slightly, her hand going to the back of her head, but stopping before touching the sutures. Corey wasn't a complainer, but Thayer could tell from the set of her shoulders and a tightness around her eyes that Corey was hurting. She added three extra strength ibuprofen to the tray she had already laden with fruit, cheese, and croissants while she waited for the bacon to finish.

By the time she made it outside with the tray and more coffee, Corey had wandered down to the dock and was peering into the glassy surface. Thayer shielded her eyes to watch her lithe, athletic body crouching to get closer to something she had spied beneath the surface. She radiated strength and vitality on every level. Thayer doubted she even knew how much.

"There are fish." Corey straightened, delighted with her discovery.

"Yes." Thayer laughed. "Plenty."

Corey picked her way back up to the deck with her bare feet. "Do you fish?"

"I can bait a hook if that's what you mean." Thayer refilled Corey's cup from the carafe she'd brought out. "I grew up spending my summers here. That's how I know Dana Fowler. We're childhood friends. We helped Nana in the gardens and picked out worms for fishing in the evenings. There's tackle in the shed." She nodded to one of the out buildings.

Corey's gaze never wavered from her. "You have hidden depths, Dr. Reynolds."

Thayer breathed a laugh. "If that's what you call perch fishing with your grandmother."

"What's her name by the way?"

Thayer's mouth quirked. "Lillian Thayer."

"Ah, so you're the namesake. That's very cool. So where is she?" Corey settled back in one of the chairs with her coffee and a handful of cheese and bacon.

Thayer sighed. "She had a stroke a couple of years ago. She recovered but she lost sight in her right eye and partial paralysis on the entire side." She looked over the lake. "Oh, before I forget, take these." She handed Corey the pain meds.

"Thanks." Corey tossed them into her mouth and washed them back with coffee. "I'm sorry; that must have been very hard for someone so independent."

"Yes, it was incredibly hard. She tried to stay out here for a while. We had some home care nurses coming out every day. We even tried having one move in, but Nana is a force of nature and pretty much drove them all away. One at gunpoint."

"Badass."

"I was in residency in the city and couldn't get out here and my parents are out of the country."

"Where?"

"My father's mother is Cuban and she's moved back there. My folks moved back when her health started failing."

"You're Cuban."

"A quarter, I guess, but I've only been over there twice, and I was pretty young. So culturally not at all." She nodded and popped a strawberry into her mouth. "Anyway, she really needed to be in assisted living."

"Hmm." Corey raised an eyebrow. "Bet that went over well."

Thayer blew out a breath. "Yeah, it was a mess. There was no way she was selling this place, and well, I won't bore you with the gory details, but in the end I offered to come back here for the fellowship, live in the house, and help her get settled in a very nice, private, assisted living residence not far from here. The house is taken care of and I'm able to visit her often and bring her back here when I have a few days off."

Corey smiled. "That's wonderful that you were able to make that work for her."

She grimaced. "It almost didn't work. I didn't get offered the fellowship, initially, but Nana actually knows someone on the board from when she used to volunteer at the hospital. She pulled some strings."

Corey eyed her. "It's not what you know but who you know, huh?"

She eyed her back with a teasing smile. "I assure you, I am more than qualified for the position. I was just late to apply and almost missed my window."

Corey chewed her lip, her brow furrowing. "For how long?"

"How long what?"

"How long are you here for?"

"Ah." Thayer nodded in understanding. "Well, the fellowship position is just the year." A flicker of disappointment flashed across Corey's face. "But, aside from the stroke, Nana is strong as an ox and I'm not going to abandon her. I expect to be able to parlay this position into a permanent one. They are expecting some retirements in the department within the year."

Corey made no attempt to hide her smile as she relaxed back in her chair.

Thayer sighed, afraid to look at her watch, but she knew she had to get moving. She couldn't remember the last time she had enjoyed herself this much with someone, sharing a meal, sunshine, and conversation.

Corey must have sensed her shift in attitude. "What's wrong?"

"I have to get ready for work," she admitted, finally checking the time. "I was able to shift some things around to get the morning off to stay home."

"I'm sorry." Corey stiffened. "I didn't realize. I didn't even think about it."

"Don't apologize. There was nowhere I wanted to be more than right here with you." Corey frowned, looking unsettled and Thayer wasn't sure how to make it better. "Listen, let me—"

"I've imposed enough already. I'll grab a ride to the hospital with you and get my truck." She pushed herself to her feet.

"Uh, no." Thayer pinned her with a look, standing to meet her eyes. "Sorry, forgot to mention one of the rules. No driving."

"Well." Corey stared at her. "What am I supposed to do? Stay here?"

Thayer smiled, letting her gaze suffuse with desire, and stepped closer, their bodies almost touching, her gaze lowering to Corey's lips, her intent clear. "I think that's a fine idea."

"Thayer." Corey's breath hitched. "What are you doing?"

She moved in, brushing her lips against Corey's in the softest, sweetest kiss. "I'm trying to tell you…" Thayer ghosted over her lips again, "…how very fine it would be if you stayed."

Corey sighed softly and parted her lips, her hands slipping around Thayer's waist. "I'm listening."

Thayer deepened the kiss, her tongue tasting Corey's lips as her hands slid over her shoulders and up behind her head.

Corey jerked away with a hiss, her face tight with pain as she put a hand to the back of her head.

"Oh, shit." Thayer's eyes widened in horror, realizing what she'd done. She reached for her. "Oh, Corey, I'm sorry. Let me see."

"It's okay. It's okay." Corey's attempt at a smile was far more a wince and she stepped out of Thayer's reach. "I'm fine."

Thayer crossed her arms and felt miserable as the weight of their situation, why Corey was here and what had happened last night, came crashing back around them. The reality was written in Corey's expression—frustration, anger, and pain. "What can I do?"

"What? No, this has been the best, worst first date ever." Corey smiled thinly. "Um, but I should probably just get home and rest, right?"

Thayer swallowed hard. "I'll take you wherever you want to go, but please don't drive or go home by yourself until the police tell you it's okay."

CHAPTER FIFTEEN

Corey stared out the window, wishing she could think of something to say that didn't sound trite or childish. Thayer had taken care of her, welcomed her into her home, shared herself and things that were important to her. Then she kissed her, very clearly expressing her desire for more. It had been amazing and surreal. Then it all went to shit and Thayer felt badly and Corey acted like an ass—as usual.

She felt skittish and uncertain, her relationship insecurities reared their heads again, and if that weren't enough, she had been attacked in her place of work. She was confused and angry and had texted Collier to meet her when he was available.

"Where can I take you?" Thayer broke the silence finally.

"Old Bridge Coffee House. Rachel works there and I can hang with her until Collier is free to meet me." Now that she had her wits about her, she had some questions and she wanted answers.

They were quiet again for a long time, the tension growing heavier as Thayer pulled up in front of the coffee shop and parked. "I've done something wrong but I'm not sure what." She didn't look at her.

"No. No, you haven't. You took care of me."

Thayer shook her head. "I did my job."

"And you usually take your patients home with you and make them breakfast?"

Thayer pressed her lips together. "Then what? What happened?"

Corey breathed deeply, her hand going to her chest as it tightened. "You remember the first time we saw each other?"

"Of course, it was only a few days ago."

"Right." She sucked in another breath. She couldn't wrap her head around how much had happened in such a short time. "Well, I was involved with someone—"

"Oh, my god. You have a girlfriend. Oh, god, of course you do." Thayer's head dropped to the steering wheel. "Wait. You have a girlfriend?" She shot up in her seat, eyes flashing hotly.

Corey couldn't help a laugh. "I said *was*." She placed a hand on Thayer's arm. "She left me that night."

Her head dropped against the seat, her eyes rolling to Corey. "She left you the day we met? How does that make things better? Oh, my god. I am such an idiot."

She fought a laugh. "Thayer, please, just let me explain. This is making my head hurt."

Thayer nodded, looking away again.

"We had been together…" Corey hesitated. "No, not together but dating for several months. I knew from the start she wasn't the one, but Anna is successful, bright, beautiful, and I don't know." She raked her hands through her hair making it stand up. "She wanted it, I think, and I just didn't. Not with her."

Thayer turned to her, giving Corey her full attention.

She sighed. "But instead of just ending it, I let it drag on, kept her interested somehow, and was too damn careless and lazy until she just gave up."

"And you're hurt? Sad? Angry?" Thayer attempted to fill in the blanks.

"No." Corey laughed, humorlessly. "None of those things. I'm ashamed and regretful and disappointed, but I'm not even remotely sad and I don't miss what we had—or didn't have—at all."

Thayer was quiet for a moment. "What are you trying to tell me?"

"I don't know. That I'm a heartless asshole?"

Thayer stared at her a beat before a smile split her face and she succumbed to outright laughter. "Corey Curtis, I've known you for only a few days, but I can assure you, you are anything but heartless and unequivocally, not an asshole."

Corey eyed her, fighting a smile of her own. "You don't know."

"Oh, I know." Thayer nodded, emphatically. "You may behave like an asshole, on occasion, but that is a very different business." Her mouth quirked. "And, by the way, you don't have the corner on that market. You'll find out if you want."

"Find out how?"

"Find out if you take a chance on us."

"Us?"

"I haven't been involved with anyone in a long time. Sometimes I was just too busy but mainly there hasn't been anyone who turned my head. No, that's not true. Plenty of women turn my head. There's never been anyone who exhilarates me. Not the way you do. You are a remarkable woman, Corey Curtis."

"Exhilarates. Wow." Corey had never been described like that.

"There's something between us, Corey. I know you feel it too." Thayer held her gaze. "But I'm not crazy. I don't need a U-Haul or commitment or even exclusivity if that's not what you want—at least, not right now."

Her eyes flashed with heat. "So, just sex, then?"

Thayer sucked in a breath through her teeth and shook her head. "Walked right into that one, didn't I?"

"What if I'm a shitty lay?" Corey arched a teasing brow. "At least I make you laugh, right?"

Thayer matched her gaze. "I guess I'll just have to be good enough for the both of us."

"Damn, woman." She exhaled, fighting a smile. "What was that about not doing anything to elevate my heart rate?"

Thayer smiled and shrugged. "Like you said, I didn't get where I am by being a bottom."

Corey coughed a laugh. "That's not what I said."

"I'm paraphrasing." Thayer grinned at her. "Will you check in later and let me know how you're doing and what Jim has to say about last night?"

Corey's face fell at the thought of getting back to reality. She wanted to stay in her safe and sexy bubble with Thayer a while longer. "Yeah, I will. Have inhaler will travel and I have your number, now."

"And I have yours." Thayer winked. "Take it easy today."

Corey lowered herself into one of the ratty overstuffed chairs necessary at every hipster coffeehouse. She was grateful one was available when her head started pounding again. She rested it gingerly against the back of the chair.

"What the hell happened to you?" Rachel stood over her and held out a coffee. "And what the hell are you wearing?"

She cracked an eye. "Thayer's clothes."

"No shit." Rachel dropped into a chair across from her and scooted closer. "That was fast."

She struggled up in her chair and took the offered coffee. "Regretfully, it's not like that."

"What's it like, then? You look terrible."

"Thank you. I'll sum up. Last night as I ran back into the morgue to grab my phone before I went to get Thayer for our first official date, a smelly dude cracked my head open from behind with a brick and ransacked the morgue. Oh, and he dumped an entire five-gallon box of formalin that essentially poisoned me." She stopped to take a breath and a sip of her coffee and glanced at Rachel, whose eyes were bugging out of her head.

"Anyway, Thayer found me when I failed to meet her, ripped my clothes off—we both agree we would have preferred that happen under different circumstances—and got me to the ED and treated. I have an undisclosed number of stitches in the back of my head." She turned so Rachel could see the wound. "And temporarily damaged lungs that make it hard to breathe sometimes."

"Shit, Corey. Are you okay?"

"I will be." She offered a smile to her friend to back up her claim. "But don't count on a rematch for a few days."

"Yeah, sure, no worries." Rachel looked very worried. "Who was the smelly dude?"

"I don't know." Corey glanced up as someone towered over them. "But here's the man who's going to find out, I hope."

Rachel glanced up, then rocketed out of the chair, her face paling. "Sergeant Collier."

Collier's eyes narrowed. "Ms. Wiley."

Corey looked between them. "You two know each other?"

"I wouldn't say *know*," Rachel muttered.

"We don't need to be introduced."

"Can I get you something?"

"Coffee, black." He sat in her vacated chair.

"Corey?" Rachel asked.

"Actually, if you have any ibuprofen or something that would be great."

"How many?"

"All of them in the world." She eased back down in the chair.

"I'll see what I can do."

CHAPTER SIXTEEN

Collier sipped the coffee Rachel had dropped off for him. "Aren't you going to ask how we know each other?"

"No." Corey tipped her head back and dropped four tablets into her mouth, washing them back with coffee. "Because I know you're not going to tell me and I'm too tired to fight about it."

He eyed her. "Are you doing okay?"

"Oh, don't get all weepy on me, Collier." She waved him off. "I'll get it out of Rachel another time."

"Right." He harrumphed and pulled his notebook from his pocket. "I trust your night went well?"

"Super." She let her head rest against the back of the chair again.

He studied her. "What's with the attitude, Curtis?"

"Attitude?" She snapped her head forward and regretted the movement instantly, her hand coming to rest against the back of her neck. "How about some jerk off nearly caved my head in outside my own goddamn office and I have no idea why?"

"Take it easy," he grumbled, gesturing to her. "Still hurt?"

"Yeah, it fucking hurts. Will you stop trying to pretend you care about me and do your job?"

He gaped at her, jerking back in his seat. She had never spoken to him like that. They had their grumpy banter and they gave each other shit whenever possible, but they did care and respect each other.

She sighed, massaging the back of her neck and let her head hang forward. "Shit, Collier. I'm sorry. I didn't mean that."

He sat back and stared. "You sure you're not brain damaged?" His mouth twisted into a smile. "Don't think you've ever apologized to me."

She knew she was forgiven but she still felt terrible. "Maybe. I don't know what the hell I'm doing right now. I'm not even wearing a bra." She caught his gaze dart to her chest and grinned at him.

"You're fucking hilarious." He reddened and flipped his book open. "I'm not going to bullshit you, Curtis."

"I expect nothing less."

"There's not much to go on. We have the brick but we're not going to get any prints off that. Officers dusted the morgue and pulled prints off just about everything. But without a suspect to match them to, there's nothing to run against. We would have to eliminate half the medical staff first. It was too late for anyone to be around to witness anything, and we've interviewed just about everyone who works in the basement and in and around the loading dock. And you didn't get a look at him. He may have had a car parked somewhere or he may have been on foot." He looked a question to her.

"I didn't see a car when I pulled in. I would have noticed."

"And what we were able to pull from the security footage confirms that. Cameras were pointed toward the loading docks, not the morgue door, but they caught a glimpse of a figure like you described. Tech guys are trying to clean it up but it doesn't look good," he explained. "So I'm thinking it was just a crime of opportunity."

She didn't like that conclusion. It made no sense. "He wouldn't have known which way cameras were pointing and if someone wanted to get into the hospital, there's half a dozen entrances he could have gone in without going through me. And what the hell are you going to ransack the morgue for?"

"So, we're back to you. Anything you can think of? You piss anyone off lately? Besides me, I mean? What about your ex?" He sat back and drank his coffee.

"I can assure you it was not my ex," she stated.

"Her father? Brother? Jilted lover?"

"No, no and no."

"All right. Listen. I'll leave it open for a few days and see if something turns up. Check other assaults and break-ins in the area and see if we get a hit on something that matches."

"Thanks." She wasn't happy about it but she knew he would do everything he could.

"In the meantime I went by your place last night and again this morning. It's clear so you can go home. It's very you by the way."

Corey straightened. "You were in my condo? How?"

He fished her keys and hospital ID from his pocket and passed them over. "Your doc gave me these last night and told me where you live. Course I could have found out on my own. I wanted to be sure it was safe."

She smiled appreciatively, chagrined at her earlier outburst. "Thank you."

"Anything else you need right now?" He stuck his notebook back in his pocket.

"Can you give me a ride to the morgue? I want to check out the damage and I need to get my truck."

"Yeah, come on."

They both got out of the car and she looked across the hood to him. "You don't need to come in. I'm fine."

"Don't flatter yourself. I want to know if you think anything was taken."

"Ladies first, then." She held the door for him grandly and he snorted a laugh.

"Well?" he asked as soon as they set foot inside.

She looked around with dismay. The floor had been cleaned but the smell of formalin lingered. All her instruments and supplies had been picked up and stacked unceremoniously on every available counter. "Shit." She picked up the Stryker saw. "Fucker busted my new saw."

"Anything missing?"

She raked her hands through her hair, wincing when she came too close to the wound. "Not that I can tell, but honestly, I don't even know everything I have down here."

Someone leaned on the buzzer at the loading dock, startling them both.

"I got it," he said, ducking back through the door. He returned a few minutes later with a very agitated Jude. "You know this little shit?"

"Corey, thank you, Jesus." He glared at Collier. "I need the body of your guy, Akers, from the construction site. His wife wants the funeral tomorrow. I've been calling you all morning. I don't even know if we can pull this off."

"Yeah, sure." She slapped on her borrowed flip-flops over to the cooler.

"What is it? Casual Friday or something?" Jude snickered, eyeing her clothes.

"Or something." She wheeled Gordon Akers's body out and helped transfer him to the funeral home stretcher. "Hold on. I have some of his stuff."

"No time," Jude replied and whipped the stretcher through the door. "Thanks, man."

"Who the hell was that little snot?" Collier grumbled.

"Jude Weatherly from the funeral home." Her lips twitched. "Why? What did he say to you?"

"Nothing I care to repeat." He headed to the door. "Let's get out of here. You look like you could use a nap."

CHAPTER SEVENTEEN

Corey took Collier's suggestion and flopped onto her bed after texting Thayer she was given the all clear to head home and that she was all right. She slept for the rest of the day and was surprised to find the sun setting when she finally cracked her eyes. Her headache was gone, and as she took a deep breath, there was no more burning in her lungs. She was, however, in desperate need of another shower.

She could not abide anything less than a scalding hot shower, so this time she turned the fan on and left the door open to dissipate any steam that might cause her breathing issues to resurface. Her shower was hot and uneventful, and for that, she was grateful. She was pulling on lounge pants and a long-sleeved Star Wars T-shirt when her doorbell chimed. She took the stairs two at a time thinking Collier would bust it open if she didn't answer in a timely fashion.

"You made your point." She flung the door wide. "You care." She froze seeing Thayer standing at her door. "Hi. Sorry. I thought you were someone else."

"Well, I do care," Thayer replied, "which is why I've been texting you all afternoon and evening. And then I got worried. And then I bought dinner and brought it over so I would have an excuse to check in on you. Are you hungry?" She held up a pizza box.

"Yeah." Corey nodded, enthusiastically. "Actually, I haven't eaten since the last time you fed me so this makes perfect sense." She moved back from the door and relieved Thayer of the pizza. "Come on in." She headed to the kitchen, grateful she had straightened up yesterday.

"I hope you're okay with bacon cheeseburger pizza. It's kind of my jam after a long day." Thayer slid onto a stool on the opposite side of the kitchen counter.

"Okay with it? Marry it, more like." She paused. "Why do you know someone who isn't?"

"Actually, yes, and it doomed our relationship."

"Well, yeah. How could it not? There is no compromising on pizza toppings."

Thayer narrowed her eyes. "Green pepper?"

"Amazing."

"Onions?"

"Always."

"Pineapple?"

"The best."

"Mushrooms?"

Corey hesitated. "I can pick them off."

"Black olives?"

She grinned. "Verboten."

Thayer's mouth twitched. "Not a deal breaker, I suppose."

Corey dropped her head onto her hands. "Oh, thank god." She sighed before lunging for the pizza box and helping herself to the biggest slice. She crammed a huge bite into her mouth. "Mmm, so good."

Thayer laughed and chose a slice for herself. "So, it seems we're not doomed."

"Were you concerned?"

Thayer chewed thoughtfully. "Your truck is out front."

"It is?" She feigned surprise. "Huh."

Thayer arched a brow at her and continued to eat. "You drove AMA."

"Advanced maternal age? Isn't that thirty-five?" She took another bite and looked away.

"Clever. Against medical advice. But I see you're up on your acronyms."

"Thayer, I'm fine." Corey grinned. "What would you like to drink?" She opted to change the subject and turned to the fridge, flinging it open. "I have beer and uh, tap water." She turned with two bottles.

Thayer, her mouth full, waved her over and took a bottle, twisting the cap, and draining half of it to wash down her pizza.

"Hidden depths, Dr. Reynolds."

Thayer raised her bottle. "If that's what you call enjoying a good lager, sure."

She raised her bottle to her lips and paused. "I'm okay to drink this, right?"

"Absolutely not. No booze."

"Oh." She set it on the counter, eyeing it longingly.

"Corey, I'm joking."

She snatched it back up and took a long pull. "Okay, good."

"There's something I need to tell you." Thayer's face grew serious but her eyes danced with humor.

"Uh-oh." She lowered her bottle. "Sounds ominous."

"It may be. That black A4, you know the one?" She grinned. "It belongs to Dr. Tweedle."

Corey's jaw dropped. "No way." Her face split in a huge grin. "Holy shit."

Thayer nodded. "We all got an email reminder from security to park in lit areas, lock your car doors and call on security to walk you to your car if you're feeling unsafe because there was an attempted late night break in."

Corey cracked up. "Oh, shit. That is so funny. I'm going to laugh about that forever." She reached for her beer again. "Wonder what he was doing there so late."

"Probably his secretary."

She choked on her beer. "Really?"

"I don't know." Thayer laughed. "I just made that up. Don't repeat that."

Corey watched as Thayer spun on her chair to survey her living room. It was nothing fancy but the furniture matched and was comfortable. She had an entertainment center against one wall with her television, Blue Ray collection and some of her favorite books. All other walls were adorned with framed movie posters from the eighties—her favorites—that her best babysitter, a woman with whom she still kept in touch and considered a friend, introduced her to.

Thayer hopped off the stool and worked her way around for a closer look. "I don't even know most of these." She stopped in front of the poster of *9 to 5*. "Is that Dolly Parton?"

"And Jane Fonda and Lily Tomlin. You've never seen it?" She was aghast.

"Uh-oh." Thayer glanced at her. "Doom isn't threatening again is it?"

"Oh, no. Your eighties movie education is something easily corrected."

"Phew." Thayer moved on and pointed to the poster of *Aliens*. "This one I know."

"That's a start."

"This one looks ridiculous." Thayer tapped on the glass. "I mean this woman is gorgeous but what is she wearing? A wetsuit?"

"That, my friend, is Helen Slater as Billie Jean Davy and *The Legend of Billie Jean* is amazing and I used to want to be her. I credit her with helping make me the woman I am today."

"Wow, that's high praise. Guess I'll have to give it a fair shot."

"Fair is fair." Corey grinned stupidly.

Thayer smiled back but clearly didn't get the joke. "So, it looks like I have my work cut out for me." She eyed the many other posters.

"I can send you home with some if you like."

"First, I don't have a television. It's on my list of things to do." She turned and faced her. "Second, why would I want to watch your favorite movies without you?"

Corey's heart skipped a beat at Thayer's clear intention to come over more often. Her brain quickly flashed images of the two of them cuddled on the couch together...and then doing other things. Thayer turned those golden eyes on her and she lost herself again in the fantasy of Thayer under her, over her, inside her. Her brain shorted out as her muscles tightened and her core flooded with heat and a delicious ache between her legs. "Okay," she blurted, finally wrestling herself back to reality.

"But not tonight," Thayer said regretfully, breaking her gaze as if she could read her mind. "I have to go in again and do an overnight and I want to hear what the police said about your assault last night."

Corey's face fell as, once again, reality beat her into submission. She dropped onto the sofa and flung her long legs on the ottoman. "My assault," she grumbled. "Jesus, that pisses me off."

Thayer sat next to her on the sofa but perched on the edge so she could look at her. "I'm sorry. I didn't mean to upset you."

"No, it's not you." She reached out and placed a hand on her arm. "It just makes me sound like such a victim." She blew out a breath. "Which I am, I guess."

"Could Jim tell you anything?"

"Only how slim the chances are of ever finding the asshole."

Thayer looked concerned. "Do you want to talk it out? See if something else comes to mind?"

She managed a small smile at Thayer's offer to help her gain back control. She was thoughtful and perceptive and it touched Corey deeply. "I don't know what else I can add."

"Well, what do you keep in the morgue?"

"Dead bodies and body parts, paperwork about bodies and parts and instruments with which to dissect bodies and parts."

"Could he have been looking for a body?"

"In the drawers?"

"Okay, stupid question. What about something that came in with a body? Drugs or money?"

That got Corey's attention and she cocked her head. "Seems plausible but anything like that usually gets snapped up by police long before the body ever gets to me. There have been things I've found on people, but again, the cops are the first phone call I make."

"Okay, something that wouldn't have been suspicious or meaningful to anyone else?"

"Sure, okay, but the only things I've even had all week are…" Corey trailed off and sat up.

"What?" Thayer asked with wide eyes.

"The stuff from Gordon Akers's pockets."

Thayer frowned. "The guy from the construction site the other day?"

"Yeah." Her lips pursed. "I'm still holding onto a lighter and a multi-tool. It's been locked up in the fireproof cabinet."

Thayer blew out a breath. "Seems like silly things to hurt someone over."

Corey pushed herself to her feet, her brain whirling, as she grabbed her phone off the kitchen counter and swiped it on. She searched for a few minutes before looking up, chewing on her lip in thought. "When is your shift over tomorrow?"

"Eight in the morning," Thayer answered, suspiciously. "But I'll need to crash for a while after. Why?"

"Do you want to go somewhere with me at six?" She raised her brows, hopefully. "It'll be fun."

Thayer stood and crossed her arms like she sensed something was about to happen. "Okay," she hesitated. "What's the occasion?"

"A funeral."

CHAPTER EIGHTEEN

Thayer cracked up in full-throated laughter for several seconds before noticing Corey's expectant expression. "You're serious?"

"Fun, right?"

"Wow. You really know what a woman wants. Would we consider it a first date, then?" She laughed again. "Because that's a story to tell the children."

Corey's eyes lit up. "You want kids?"

"Focus, woman."

"Can I explain?"

Thayer gestured grandly. "Please do. I can't wait."

"Okay, but could you maybe wait for a minute or two? Maybe longer. You are so beautiful when you're fiery. If you don't kiss me I may go crazy."

Thayer's blood heated immediately at the thought. The same thought she had the moment she arrived. But Corey's simple, heartfelt non sequitur and the desire clear in her eyes cut right to Thayer's core. "Because you're not crazy, already?"

she teased, gaining a second to compose herself but unable to tear her eyes away from her.

Corey closed the distance between them, stopping just short of touching her. "Oh no, I definitely am."

She was so close Thayer could feel her breath on her face, smell her soap and feel the warmth radiating from her body. "Is this a ploy to get me to agree?"

"No." Corey inched closer, their lips brushing. "Is it working?"

"Yes." Thayer sighed and closed her mouth over Corey's, tentative at first, until she felt Corey's hands slide around her waist and heard a soft moan of pleasure, from which one of them she was unsure.

Kissing Corey was knee-weakening and when she parted her lips, Corey took the lead, and Thayer knew for certain the next groan was from her. She slipped her hands up Corey's strong arms and over her shoulders, partly to get closer and partly to steady herself as their kiss deepened, tongues coming out to play.

Their bodies molded together, breasts pressed against one another, as their heads jockeyed for position, breathing and heart rates accelerating rapidly as they toyed with and tested each other. Her body reacted dramatically, belly tightening and center dampening, when Corey's hands slid up her back, her fingers threading through her hair, pinning her in place and devouring her mouth with passion.

Thayer let herself go for another moment before she got a hand between them and pushed against Corey's chest. "Stop. Stop. Corey, stop," she said, breathlessly.

Corey froze for an instant before she disentangled herself, backing away, quickly. "I'm sorry." She looked stricken. "I'm sorry. I thought you wanted...I thought...oh, shit."

"No. No. I did, I mean, I do. You thought right. That was, I mean, you are...oh, god." Heat rose to her face as she trailed off, knowing she sounded ridiculous.

"What?" Corey whispered, her voice husky.

Thayer pulled away further and sat down in the armchair, the only place Corey wouldn't be able to be near her. She pulled her thoughts together with effort. "I can't do this with you—wait." She held up a hand at Corey's crushed expression. "Let me finish. I can't do this with you unless I can stay, and I can't stay tonight. I'm not here for a quickie, as amazing as that sounds. I want dinner and multiple orgasms and shower sex and morning sex and breakfast—in that order."

Corey's eyes bugged out of her head, her jaw dropping comically. "Sweet Jesus."

Thayer sat back in her chair and crossed her legs. Her skin was sticky with arousal, but she had herself back under control. "Are you as wet as I am right, now?" She taunted Corey with hooded eyes.

Corey smiled slyly and lowered herself back onto the sofa. "Come over here and find out."

Thayer laughed. "Touché."

"You are setting the bar very high. Like bodice-ripping, romance-novel high."

"Too high?"

Corey regarded her for a moment. "No."

Somehow that simple look and one small word said with confidence sent Thayer into a tailspin again and her desire flared. "Tell me about the funeral," she blurted.

"Sure." Corey cleared her throat. "All right, I know this is going to sound totally nuts, and I don't have it sorted out in my head, but just hear me out."

"I'm listening."

"Gordon Akers's death was recorded as accidental from a fall of five stories down an airshaft at the construction site where he worked. Dr. Webster signed the death certificate based on my post or part of it. When I documented the skull fractures, I noticed a depressed linear fracture, also known as a signature fracture, inconsistent with the multiple stellate and comminuted fractures from his head cracking open like an egg when he hit bottom. There was also a curvilinear laceration in the skin corresponding to one end of the fracture." Corey paused to make sure Thayer was following.

"You think he bounced off something on the way down?"

"I did, yes," Corey agreed. "Cin and I went out to the construction site to—"

"You did what?"

"It was fine." Corey waved her off. "The site was closed and we wanted to see the airshaft for ourselves and see if we could get a picture that explained the fracture."

"And?"

"And we didn't find anything." Corey shrugged. "Nothing to explain the injury."

"And?" Thayer wasn't sure where this was going.

"Let me back up a little. It was assumed that he was hanging over the airshaft to smoke after everyone left. There was a lighter and crushed pack of cigarettes at the bottom of the shaft with him. A lot of the guys smoked, and he had been a smoker. But he was wearing both a nicotine patch and had nicotine gum wrappers in his pocket when I saw him."

Thayer considered this but wasn't clear on the mystery. "Have you ever had to quit smoking?"

"I have, actually," Corey admitted. "This body has been far from a temple."

"So, you know how hard it is."

"Yeah, I know," Corey conceded. "I get that. But what if it's not his lighter?"

"So he borrowed it."

She huffed a breath. "No. What if it wasn't an accident? What if he was killed first, then dropped down the airshaft to cover up a murder, one easily explained by smoking in the airshaft? Except he wasn't smoking, so whoever did it had to toss his smokes and lighter in with the body?"

Thayer stared at her, trying to wrap her head around everything Corey was telling her. Part of her wanted to laugh it off and the other wanted to be supportive. She opted for the latter. "And he came looking for his lighter yesterday because that links him to Gordon Akers's death?"

Corey held out her hands. "Is it any more crazy than some random guy walking by and smacking me with a brick?" Corey jerked. "A brick. Where did the brick come from?"

"A construction site?" Thayer offered, unsure whether she should be excited or afraid since that made a certain kind of sense. "Did you run any of this by Jim?"

"No. I mean, it only just occurred to me. The smoking thing bothered me, and I told him about the inconsistent fracture, but he was only going to look at the case again if Dr. Webster initiated something and he didn't."

"And Jim was okay with you going to the site?" Thayer eyed her.

"He doesn't know about that part," Corey confessed sheepishly.

"So, why go to his funeral?"

"To return his lighter."

Thayer considered all this information. "You're counting on someone knowing if it's his lighter or not."

"Exactly."

"And if it's not?"

"I'll bug Collier again about it."

"Okay, but again, what if he just borrowed someone's lighter? And if he was trying to quit, he may not have been carrying one."

Corey frowned. "I don't know. But trying to quit or not, who carries a pack of smokes but needs to borrow a lighter?"

"Someone who lost their lighter? Someone whose lighter ran out of fuel?"

"Gah." Corey threw up her hands. "Do you want to come with me tomorrow or not?"

Thayer grinned. "I do."

CHAPTER NINETEEN

"Will you relax, please?" Thayer covered Corey's hand that was tapping out an incessant beat on the gearshift. "What are you so worried about?"

"We are about to crash the funeral of a guy I posted," Corey replied nervously. "You don't think that's weird?"

"Of course, it's weird. And probably violates half a dozen privacy laws. And it was your idea, remember?"

"Right." Corey started tapping again. "Its just crowds of strangers make me a little uncomfortable. No one goes into my line of work because they are a people person, you know?"

Thayer pursed her lips. "Is that your way of asking me to do the talking?"

"Yes. People are drawn to you. You're charming and beautiful and you're sexy as hell."

"Oh, I get it. The truth comes out. You objectify me and only want me for my body."

"What?" Corey looked at her. "That's crazy talk. I only want you for your money and your lake house."

Thayer laughed and ran her hand up Corey's thigh. "You look sexy as hell, by the way." She inched her hand a little higher.

"Thanks," Corey yelped and jerked the wheel. She had stared at her closet so long she felt like she was going on a date. She finally decided black jeans would not look out of place at the house of a construction foreman and a midnight blue button-down would be respectful and comfortable.

Her gaze flicked to Thayer, looking gorgeous in charcoal dress pants and a dark green blouse. "You look great too."

They pulled onto the street in the blue-collar end of town, pickup trucks lining both sides as far as the eye could see.

"And I was worried we'd stand out," Corey mused.

They slowly cruised past the house, a well maintained but older two-story, clusters of men standing on the front porch and across the front lawn smoking and drinking canned beer.

Thayer glanced down at her clothes. "I'm afraid that may still be the case."

They were fortunate someone was pulling out halfway down the block and Corey easily pulled into the giant spot left behind a truck twice the size of hers. "Ready?"

"Let's do it."

Corey pulled the two items she had fetched from the morgue that morning, still in plastic bags, from the center console.

The humid summer air was so heavy with smoke, she tried to hold her breath as they made their way up the path to the front porch. All eyes were on Thayer with a few glances flicked Corey's way as they walked past. Corey tensed but fortunately they had enough respect not to catcall at a memorial service. She nearly laughed, though, when she saw a young guy gearing up to whistle before he got an elbow to his ribs from his buddy. Thayer, for her part, was as cool as usual, even smiling casually at a couple men gaping at her.

Before Corey had a chance to knock the door was flung open by a woman about her age who glared past them at the men. "Those clowns didn't give you any trouble did they?" She was blond, tiny, and very pregnant.

"Perfect gentlemen all of them," Thayer said loudly enough for the ones on the porch to hear, causing some good-natured laughter and conversation to resume.

"I'm Shelby Akers." She extended her hand with a smile. "Gordon Jr.'s wife."

"Corey Curtis." Corey met her grasp, impressed with her grip.

"Thayer Reynolds." She shook her hand. "We're very sorry for your loss."

"Thank you." Shelby's lips pressed together thinly. "It's been real hard on everyone." Her gaze flicked over their shoulders again. "You ladies better come inside, or those fools will never leave." She led them into the worn but well-appointed home, which was also filled with friends and family drinking and snacking around a buffet table. "So, how did you know Gord?"

As promised Thayer took the lead. "We didn't really, and I hope we're not intruding, but we're from the hospital and we have a couple of personal items that were left there that we wish to return to his family."

"Oh?" Shelby looked surprised. "I had thought the police brought everything after, um, you know."

Corey decided she wasn't going to let Thayer do all the work. "They were discovered later in his pockets. Is his wife around? We can give them to her."

Shelby looked sad at the mention of her. "Gloria's gone upstairs to lie down. This has all been really overwhelming. Gord was going to retire soon. They were real smart with their money and had plans to travel and do all these bucket list things while they were still young, you know?"

"I'm sorry," was all Corey could think to say.

"Let me go find JR and Dave." She turned away and immediately spun back. "Please, help yourself to a drink. I may be a minute."

Corey jumped when Thayer's fingers laced through hers and squeezed. "See, it is a date." She winked. "Can I buy you a beer?" She released Corey's hand and moved to the table in front of them with ice-filled buckets of beer.

Corey wanted to make a joke but she wanted a drink more. "God, yes."

Thayer popped open two Bud Lights and handed one to her, taking a sip and smacking her lips. "Ahhh."

Corey hid her smile behind her beer and took several long swallows. "Best Bud ever," she agreed, grateful there was no one within earshot but still aware of the attention Thayer attracted. Just about everyone was casting glances her way except for a big guy in jeans and a plaid shirt who was heading fast through the front door. Corey caught the whiff of stale smoke behind him and figured he was heading out for a fix. It occurred to her that she would have to get used to the staring just as Thayer clearly had. She would have to examine that more another time.

After a few minutes Shelby wended back through the milling mourners trailed by two men of similar age who were clearly brothers, and who, if Corey squinted, resembled what she imagined Gordon Akers may have looked like.

"JR, Dave, this is Corey and Thayer from the hospital." She gestured to each of them.

Hands were shaken and pleasantries and condolences exchanged.

"She says you have something of my dad's?" the elder brother, JR, asked.

Corey dug in her pocket for the tool. "This was in his pocket when I saw him." She kept it vague as to where and when.

Dave snatched it out of her hand. "No way." He removed it from the plastic. "Remember this, JR?" he gushed enthusiastically.

His older brother stared at the tool, his lips thinning. "Yeah." His voice was thick with emotion.

"We saved up and bought this for our dad nearly twenty years ago." He handled the tool reverently. "I had no idea he still had it, never mind carried it on him." As soon as the words left his mouth he realized what he had said and tears sprang to his eyes.

Dave coughed and cleared his throat as he flipped the tool around. "We couldn't afford to get it engraved so we took a screw and scratched our initials in." He showed Corey the illegible scratch marks on one side.

Her heart clenched. "It must have been very important to him to be carrying it around after all these years." She felt Thayer reach for her hand again and give it a squeeze.

"Yeah," Dave whispered not taking his eyes off it. "Thanks for bringing it."

"Sure." Corey cleared her throat and dug in her other pocket. "I have this too." She produced the bag with the lighter.

JR frowned at it. "That's not his."

"It was with him," Corey explained.

JR took the bag but didn't remove the lighter. He studied it through the plastic. "It's not his," he said again. "Dad quit smoking five months ago when we told him we were expecting his first grandchild." He pulled Shelby in close and placed a protective hand on her abdomen. "He was doing really well with the quitting. He wanted to set a good example." His voice broke at the end.

Dave took the bag with the lighter and examined it. "Yeah, it's not his." He gave a little laugh. "Even when he was smoking, he always used those disposable plastic ones because he could open his beers with them too. Those things were always scattered all over the house with chewed up ends from bottle caps."

"I know whose it is." Shelby took the bag and flipped it around in her hand. "Gord's crew has been stopping by and visiting all week, bringing over casseroles their wives made and such. A few days ago a pack of them showed up and one guy was asking if the police had found anything with Gord or had given Gloria anything. He was kind of twitchy about it and said Gord had borrowed his lighter, but it was really important to him and his initials were engraved on it."

Corey struggled to contain her excitement and she could feel Thayer's eyes on her. "May I?" She reached for it again and held it up to the light. She was absolutely not taking it out of the bag now. On the bottom she could just make out a faint M.G. Or it could have been an O. "Do you remember his name?"

Shelby shrugged. "Mark maybe? Or Mike? I'm sorry there were so many of them, and honestly, all those guys kind of look the same to me." She glanced around the room. "I think he was here today, but I don't see him now. Maybe he's outside."

"Borrowed it, huh?" Thayer commented, eyeing Corey from the side.

"That's what he said."

"Confiscated, more like," JR added. "He was a stickler about the guys not smoking on the site. There was an area set up for them on the ground for lunch breaks and stuff. And, like I said, he quit. We were all real proud of him."

"I'll hang on to it then and see if I can get it back to him." Corey jammed it back into her pocket before anyone had a chance to disagree with her. "Thanks so much for taking the time to speak with us."

"We're very sorry about your father." Thayer smiled gently at them. "From the number of people here he was obviously dearly loved."

"Thank you." Dave grinned at her and shook her hand. "If yours was the last face dad saw I'm sure he died a happy man."

"Jesus, Davey," JR hissed.

Thayer laughed.

CHAPTER TWENTY

Corey stood in the front of the house, nearly cleared out now, watching half a dozen trucks pull away when Thayer caught up with her.

"Hey. You took off fast."

"Sorry. I wanted to see if I could find out who he is." She caught movement at the side of the house as a young guy was coming around the side, a beer in each hand. He was apparently here for the free booze.

"Hey, man." Corey strode up to him, immediately noticing his bloodshot, droopy eyes and the unmistakable smell of weed wafting off him. That explained what he was doing at the side of the house.

His eyes went wide and darted around like he was going to run.

"I just want to ask you a quick question." Corey held out a calming hand.

"Sure, yeah," he drawled.

"Do you work on the site at Coburn and Hall?"

"I do, yeah. I'm pretty new."

"Do you know a guy with the initials M.G.?"

"Um, shit, I don't know." He shrugged. "There's like thirty guys working on that site. I'm sure one of them is named Matt, Mike, or Mark." He giggled to himself. "Mark. I think it's Mark."

"Thanks." She headed for her truck.

"Anything?" Thayer was leaning against the passenger side.

"Not really." Corey unlocked the door and held it for Thayer.

"So, what now?"

Corey drummed her fingers against the steering wheel, lost in thought. She dug the bag out of her pocket and looked at it again before dropping it back into the console. "You want to do one more thing with me?" she asked, facing her.

Thayer sighed. "I don't know if I can stand any more of your first date fun. So I hope your next stop involves dinner at that little hole-in-the-wall Mexican place I've heard good things about but haven't had the chance to try."

Corey couldn't tell if she was teasing her again or if she was really starting to get annoyed with her. She reached her hand across the console and collected Thayer's in her own, lacing their fingers together. "Thank you for doing this with me."

Thayer met her gaze and reached to brush at a wisp of hair that had fallen into Corey's eyes. "You're welcome." She smiled.

Corey chewed her lip. When Thayer turned those eyes on her, she felt completely bewitched. It was all she could do not to fire up her truck and drive them straight back to her condo, or Thayer's place, or anywhere really she could wrap her arms around her and feel her against her and taste her lips. Which is why what came out of her mouth next surprised even her. "Yes, absolutely, dinner. I love that place and that's where we'll go right after we do one quick thing. I promise." She flashed what she hoped was her most charming smile.

Thayer peered through the windshield at the building, her expression troubled. "Corey, you must know by now that I am absolutely crazy for you, but I cannot in good conscience support this plan. It's trespassing. How are you even going to get in?" She gestured to the closed perimeter fence.

"Crazy for me, huh?" Her eyes danced. "That's pretty much my all-time favorite Madonna song, by the way. *Vision Quest* was kind of cheesy, though."

"Mine too, and I've seen the movie." Thayer fought a smile. "But that was not supposed to be the takeaway from what I just said."

Corey looked around the site. "Yeah, the fence was open last time but there's a gap and I can make myself small. I'll be quick. Why don't you just wait here?" She hopped out.

"What?" Thayer opened her door. "You did not just ask me to wait in the car, did you?"

She laughed. "I did nothing of the kind. You didn't want to come."

"No, I don't, and I don't want you to either, but since I can't stop you, I better go with you. Hurry up, it's getting dark." Thayer stalked toward the gap in the fence gate with Corey jogging to catch up.

Thayer kicked some loose nails around the debris-covered fifth floor. "Are you sure it's safe to be up here?" She peered through a gap in the unfinished floor that looked like it went all the way down to the bottom and was crossed with loose boards. She scooted a nail over the edge with her foot, listening for the silent seconds before she heard it plink down at the bottom.

"I'm not sure of anything." Corey was crouched in the corner, pawing through a pile of rubble. "But you're right. That lighter doesn't mean anything. He borrowed it, confiscated it, or found it. I don't know. There's still something that isn't sitting right with me about this whole thing, but Collier isn't going to take me seriously unless I have something to actually tell him that makes sense."

"What are we looking for exactly?" Thayer asked, looking around aimlessly.

"I don't know exactly." Corey sighed. "Something heavy, thin, and sort of rounded that could have been used to cave in someone's head. Like a pipe, maybe."

Thayer moved to the opposite side and kicked around some boards. "Like this?" She picked up a two-foot length of rebar. One end was darkened and crusted with sludge. "Jesus, is that blood?"

"You're going to want to put that down," a gruff voice said from behind her as something hard pressed into the back of her neck.

CHAPTER TWENTY-ONE

Corey whirled around, jumping to her feet to see a large man with a nail gun. "Hey!"

"Stay where you are unless you want me to send a three-inch steel nail through her pretty little throat," he growled, gripping Thayer at the left shoulder and driving the tip hard into the back of her neck.

Thayer winced, staggering forward at the pressure until he jerked her back upright. The length of rebar clattered to the floor at her feet and she held her hands out to her sides.

"It's you." Corey's gaze darted between his dangerously wild eyes and Thayer's wide, terrified ones. She recognized the man immediately as the one who grossed Cin out. "I know you. You attacked me in the morgue, didn't you? You killed Gordon Akers."

"I did what I had to," he barked, looking around as if he was trying to make a decision. "And now you're going to do what you have to."

Her eyes narrowed, her heart pounding. "And what's that?"

"Give me that lighter. I know you have it. I heard you say it at Gord's house."

Her gaze stayed on Thayer, who stood very still, her eyes locked onto Corey's. "I don't have it on me. It's in my truck. Let her go and I'll go get it for you."

"You think I'm stupid?" He snarled and jerked Thayer around, propelling her toward the unfinished part of the floor. There was a thick, two-foot wide board serving as a bridge to a section of scaffolding surrounding a reinforced cement column. The column rose from the ground and went straight up through to the floors yet to be constructed.

Thayer stopped at the edge, resisting, beginning to tremble visibly.

"Walk." He pressed the nail gun harder against her neck, causing her to gasp in pain.

"No." Corey started toward them. "Thayer."

"Don't move!"

"Corey, do as he says. I'll be okay." Thayer's voice wavered.

Corey watched their agonizingly slow progress across the fifteen feet to the scaffolding. The man shoved Thayer forward and she stumbled onto a small platform with a frightened cry. She scrabbled at the column, her hands closing around a large ring bolt to steady herself.

"Thayer?" Corey's heart leapt to her throat.

"I'm okay," she replied shakily. The platform was three feet wide and circled the thick column. There were no other planks that crossed to the floor but the one the man was hurrying back across.

Corey watched in horror as he jumped back to solid floor before turning with a sneer and pulling the board across with him, stranding Thayer on the platform.

"That lighter is the only thing connecting me to Akers." He jabbed a finger at Corey and hooked a thumb behind him. "And she's my insurance you'll come back with it."

Corey swallowed hard, her mind in a panic. She scanned the scaffolding. Thayer wouldn't even be able to see over the edge to the supports holding it. Maybe she could guide her down.

Thayer was watching her, a curious expression on her face. "You'll do nothing of the kind, Corey. He's already killed someone and he'll have no trouble killing us as well."

"Gord was an accident. But I ain't going back to prison." His eyes darted between Thayer and Corey.

Corey ran her hands through her hair. "Thayer, I have to do something."

"You'll get me that goddamn lighter!" he raged.

Thayer breathed a laugh. "Honey, he can't hurt me now." She pulled her phone from her pocket. "The nail gun's not going to fire nails out like bullets, like you see in the movies."

"Shut the fuck up!" His face purpled with rage and he waved the tool around uselessly, realizing his mistake. He had no leverage now.

"I'm calling the police," Thayer announced calmly as she tapped the screen with her free hand, the other holding the column.

"Make sure you ask for Sergeant Jim Collier." Corey couldn't help her triumphant grin as Thayer simply made her call. "If you still think you're getting away with this, your only chance now is to run. Nothing connects you to Akers but the lighter, the murder weapon, and the two women you just confessed to."

"I said I ain't going back." The man spun to her with unadulterated fury and charged.

Corey jumped back as he swung down at her with the nailer, raising her left arm to protect her head and swinging her right in a textbook right hook that connected solidly with his jaw just as the tool cracked down on her left forearm, the intense pain staggering her.

"Corey!" Thayer screamed helplessly from her prison.

She could already hear the sirens as she swayed, cradling her left arm to her side. "It's over." She panted. "Don't make this worse."

The man straightened, spitting blood. "I ain't got nothing to lose," he replied ominously and charged her again.

She bent her knees, lowering her center of gravity as she prepared to take the hit.

He hadn't been that far away, but he hit her with the force of a linebacker, sending them both sailing backward through the air and crashing down onto a pile of loose boards.

The air whooshed from her lungs, pain lancing through her neck and back as his weight came down on her. She swung her right elbow hard into his throat. He gurgled a horrible sound and started to get up when her knee connected solidly with his groin as he tried to scrabble away, choking and gagging.

"Corey, get out of there!" Thayer yelled.

She pushed herself up from the pile of debris, gripping a length of two-by-four in her right hand. She glanced at Thayer to make sure she was okay before her gaze trained on the man, cradling his balls and moaning pitifully as he tried to catch his breath.

She was ending this. Her left arm ached viciously but there was nothing wrong with her right as she adjusted her grip on the board and swung hard, striking him in the side of the head as he tried to limp away. "What comes around goes around, asshole."

He dropped to the floor. Corey pushed him onto his back with her foot and she could see he was breathing evenly. She looked up at Thayer and took several shuddering breaths. "Are you all right?" she panted, throwing the board to the floor.

Thayer nodded, her trembling hand going to her chest. "I'm all right. Are you?"

"Yeah. I think he broke my arm. Hold on and I'll get the plank." Corey moved to step around his body when she heard a loud crack of wood—and fell through the floor. The last thing she heard was Thayer screaming her name.

"Corey!" Thayer screamed. "Oh my god, Corey!" There was a terrifying crash of wood and a sickening thump as Corey's body landed and a dust cloud billowed up from below. Thayer dropped to her knees on the platform, angling to see to the fourth floor. Corey was on her back so close to the edge of the unfinished floor her arm was hanging over. She wasn't moving. She wasn't far away but Thayer didn't know how to get to her. The sirens wailed and lights of arriving patrol cars reflected outside but help was still precious minutes away.

Corey groaned and stirred and Thayer's heart leapt to her throat. "No, honey. Oh, god. Please stay still."

Corey's legs shifted. "Thayer?"

"Yes, honey. I'm here." She dropped to her stomach and peered beneath her. There was a plank of wood from the next lower platform to the floor beneath her. If she could climb the scaffolding, she could get to Corey. "I'm coming to you sweetheart. Please don't move."

She didn't have time to be afraid as she stayed on her belly and swung her legs over the edge, feeling for a support with her feet. As soon as her feet found purchase, she lowered herself over the edge. "Corey, talk to me. I can't see you right now, and I need to know you're all right."

"…'m hurt…"

"Oh, honey." Her chest tightened with fear at the sound of her weak voice. "I'm coming. Please, hold on. Keep talking to me." She climbed faster, dropping the last few feet to the platform at the same time she heard boots on the stairs and the identifying shouts of the police. "We're on the fourth floor." She raced across the wood plank, dropping down next to Corey. "Call an ambulance."

Jim Collier thundered up the stairs with a platoon of uniformed officers, weapons drawn. "Where is he?"

Thayer didn't spare him a glance. "One up."

He grunted, holstering his weapon and waved his officers up the stairs. He crouched down next to Thayer. "What can I do?"

"She fell through the floor." Thayer placed one arm across Corey's body and her hand gripped the edge of the floor to keep her from going over if she moved. With her other she took Corey's pulse at the wrist. It was far too fast.

She leaned over to look at her face. Her eyes were glassy and unfocused but open. Her breathing was rapid and shallow with frothy blood staining her lips. "Corey, honey, can you hear me?"

Corey blinked, "Hurts…"

"I know, honey." Thayer smoothed her hair, slick with sweat. "Tell me where."

"My head…" She panted. "…and…chest."

She unbuttoned Corey's shirt and slipped a hand inside, running it across her chest and her sides, stopping when she felt the unnatural movement of fractured ribs on the left. The touch caused Corey to cry out in agony.

"Okay. Okay." Thayer smoothed her pained brow. "I'm sorry." She turned to Collier. "Go meet the ambulance. We need a backboard and C-collar. If they can get the stretcher up here great, but if not, we'll carry her on the board. Ask someone to call ahead to the ED. We need a head and spine CT, X-ray, and give thoracic surgery a heads up that she has multiple rib fractures, at least a punctured lung, a fractured arm, and other possible internal injuries from a fall of approximately fifteen feet."

Collier winced. "So, she's a mess is what you're saying?"

"Did you get all that?" Thayer snapped.

"I got it." He turned to the stairs. "I'm going."

She looked at Corey's face. Her eyes were fluttering closed. "Corey, you need to stay awake for me now." She used her best bedside command voice.

Corey's eyes dragged open. "Trying...."

"Paramedics are on their way up." Her voice grew thick with emotion, unshed tears burning behind her eyes. "They're going to take care of you."

Corey's mouth twitched in an attempt at a smile. "You..." She panted. "Take...me home."

Thayer lost the battle against the tears and they streamed down her face. "I think I'm too close to this one, sweetheart." She was helpless to ease Corey's pain.

Corey smiled, her eyes rolling to meet Thayer's. "'m sorry..."

"For what, honey?" Thayer choked back a sob. "None of this is your fault."

"Never even took you...on a proper date..." Corey wheezed a ragged breath, blood bubbling from her mouth as her eyes rolled back in her head.

"Corey? Corey?" Thayer cried as she heard the ambulance siren come to a stop.

CHAPTER TWENTY-TWO

Corey could hear the hiss and beep of machines. She tried to open her eyes, tried to swallow, tried to speak at the sound of voices nearby, but in the end she succumbed to a heavy blackness.

She was aware, briefly, when someone was touching her, rolling her, causing her pain and she groaned her displeasure.

"I know, honey, I'm sorry," a soft voice soothed. "Almost done."

She relaxed and faded away again.

Her head pounded and it felt like a rhino was sitting on her chest. Her throat was so sore and she desperately wanted a drink. She tried to move her left arm but couldn't, and a throbbing pain tore a ragged groan from her chest.

"No. No, honey, don't try to move."

She felt a cool hand against her face and focused on forming a single word. "Water."

There was movement and the sound of water pouring. She tried to open her eyes but the bright light stabbed them closed again with a sharp gasp.

She felt a straw pressed against her lips. "Small sips," the soothing voice said. "Just a little."

Much too soon the straw was removed and she heard movement again. The lights were dimmed in the room. "I'll get your doctor."

She woke again to gentle hands prying her lids open, a sharp light piercing her eyes. "Corey, welcome back," an unfamiliar voice rumbled.

"You've been keeping everyone on their toes the last couple of days. Dr. Reynolds has been very worried and the nurses are starting to complain they keep finding your friends hanging around past visiting hours." She felt a cold stethoscope against the bare skin of her chest. "Breathe deeply for me."

She attempted an inhale, shuddering as pain wracked her chest. She tried to bring her right arm up, the only one that could move, to push him away.

"Shhh, Corey, it's okay," Thayer soothed, gripping her hand gently and holding it. "You need to try, sweetheart. Your lung collapsed and it will help to breathe deeply. I know it hurts."

"Thayer," she whispered, relaxing at the sound of her voice and struggling to open her eyes and focus on her.

The exam was finished. "You're strong," the doctor said. "You're doing well and a lot of people are looking out for you." He patted her leg. "I'll be back to see you soon. Until then you're in the best hands, I think."

A door opened and closed. She rolled her blurry eyes toward the sound. "Who?"

Thayer slid a chair over. "That was Dr. Michael Bryant. You might know him already but I just met him. You're in Critical Care but you'll probably be moved down to a room later today."

She frowned, confusion and pain were all she was sure of as she tried to make sense of the words. "Thayer?"

"Yes, hi." She sat on Corey's right. "I'm really happy to see those beautiful blue eyes." Tears glistened on her lashes.

Her hand fumbled toward Thayer's face, brushing clumsily at her cheek before Thayer gripped her hand in her own. "You're crying."

"Yeah." Thayer half laughed and half sobbed. "I can't remember the last time I cried this much."

Corey could only stare at her, her muddled mind unable to process the information. "Were we in the car? I can't remember. Did we crash? Are you hurt?"

"No, honey, I'm not hurt." Thayer pressed Corey's hand to her lips, letting the tears fall freely. "You fell through the floor at the construction site. Your left arm is fractured, you have three fractured ribs that punctured your lung, soft tissue and muscle damage to your neck and back and a severe concussion. You've been unconscious for two days."

Her fog was starting to clear but she still couldn't remember. "Is that all?" She tried to sit up.

"No. Don't." Thayer placed a hand against her shoulder. "Hold on."

There was a whirring sound and the bed lifted, raising her head. The change in position made her head swim and her stomach turn slightly. She swallowed heavily.

"Here." A plastic dish was placed under her chin and a cool hand behind her neck helping her forward. "It's okay," Thayer murmured as Corey painfully retched up the little water she'd just drank.

Thayer disappeared for a moment and returned with a cool cloth to wipe her face. "Okay?"

"Yeah." She sighed. "Shit, that hurt."

Thayer sank back down in the chair. "You're going to be okay." Her voice wavered like she was convincing herself as well. "You have a chest tube in place to drain the air and blood from your pleural space and keep your lung inflated. We don't yet know what long-term effects you may experience from your head injury. There were no skull fractures or hemorrhages but there was some swelling of your brain." Thayer frowned. "Headaches, maybe, vision problems. You may never be able to fight full contact again. Your arm will heal just fine but you may need physical therapy for your neck and back."

Corey blinked and looked at her left arm. It was propped on pillows, immobilized and wrapped in a moldable brace from her shoulder to her hand. Corey understood the words she was saying—physical therapy and head injuries—but couldn't process what it all meant for her. "Jesus, Thayer, anything else?"

"I'm sorry." Thayer shook her head. "I don't know what role to play right now." She stood and raked her hands through her tangled hair as she turned away from the bed.

Corey measured her breathing, working on inhaling fully despite the pain. "Is there any good news?" she finally asked on an exhale.

Thayer barked a hysterical laugh and turned back around, fresh tears shining in her eyes. "You scared the shit out of me, Corey."

"Are you angry with me?" Corey tried again to remember something and was rewarded with stabbing pain to her skull.

Thayer turned away again, seemingly unable to look at her. "No, of course not."

"Thayer," she whispered, feeling the pull of sleep, but pain kept her lucid as she fumbled her hand toward her. "Please come closer."

Thayer spun and immediately gripped her hand, dropping into the chair. "I'm sorry. It's been…I've been… You're here and you're awake. That's the best news. And somehow your stitches held, so there's that."

"Two days, you said." She searched Thayer's eyes. "Have you been here the whole time?"

"Is that weird?" She breathed a laugh.

Corey attempted a smile but the pain was overwhelming. "Yes." Her voice was tight, sweat prickling the skin on her face and neck. "But weird in a good way."

Thayer looked at her with concern. "Oh, honey, hold on," she said as she disappeared out the door.

Corey looked up at the ceiling and tried to remember what had happened. The last thing she vaguely recalled was being at the memorial reception with Thayer and then wanting to go back to the site.

She wondered if her memory would ever return and if she even wanted it to. It didn't seem important now and she pushed the thoughts away. Searching for memories that wouldn't surface made her feel like someone was splitting her head open with an ax.

Thayer returned with Dr. Bryant, who smiled reassuringly as he came around to the monitors on her left side. "How are you feeling, Corey?" He studied the displays for her O2 saturation, respiration, and heart rate.

"Like I fell through the floor at a construction site, I guess."

"I guess." He leaned over her and checked her pupil reactivity again. "The thing you need the most right now is rest, so we're going to help you with that." He thumbed a button on her infusion IV pump and the numbers on the display ticked up, increasing her medication.

Corey sighed deeply as the pain receded and her body felt like it was sinking into the bed. "Oh. Thanks."

"You're welcome." He smiled and disappeared again and so did she.

CHAPTER TWENTY-THREE

Thayer pulled up a chair in Corey's new private room. She hadn't awakened again, and Thayer had taken the time to go home, power nap and get dressed for work. She only had an hour now before she was on shift. She couldn't ask for another trade, and in fact, needed to start paying them back and then some. She would only be able to see Corey when the ED was slow enough for her to slip away and before and after her shifts, when she could manage.

She trailed her fingertips up and down Corey's right arm, absently tracing the tattoo of the fish and coral reef. Her mind wandered, at first darkly, as she relived the horrible moments of Corey fighting a man twice her size and then crashing through the floor as the wood gave way beneath her. Thayer swallowed hard, closing her eyes against the memories of the sound of her body hitting the floor. She had never been so scared.

She shook her head, dispelling the images and focusing on the woman in front her, alive and recovering. She finally admitted how hard she was falling for Corey.

She picked up on the change in Corey's breathing a second before her eyes fluttered as she came out from under the medications again. "Hey, tough girl." Thayer laced their fingers, giving her hand a gentle squeeze to encourage her awake.

"Hey." Corey blinked and focused on her. "You're still here."

"Of course." Thayer smiled. "Although, here is somewhere new."

"Yeah, I guess so." Corey looked around the dim room, groggily. "Will you do the thing with the bed?"

"Are you sure?"

"Yeah."

Thayer hit the button to elevate the bed, watching her carefully.

"I'm good." Corey sucked in a breath. "Keep going, please."

Thayer raised the bed to nearly a forty-five-degree angle and stopped.

"Thank you," Corey sighed.

Thayer sat back down. "How's your pain?"

"Um, distant, for now."

"Good." Thayer eyed her monitors. "They have you on a pretty powerful cocktail of antibiotics and pain meds. They've switched you to a patient-controlled analgesia pump." She showed Corey the button at the end of the long rubber wire running to the pump and her IV. "You want to hold on to it?"

"No. I can barely hold a thought right now." Corey shifted in the bed and winced. "I think you need to start calling me something else."

Thayer placed the button across Corey's lap. "What do you mean?"

"I sure as hell don't feel very tough."

Thayer watched, sympathetically, while Corey felt across her body through her gown to the chest tube in place, stitched between her ribs, and skimmed her right hand over the heavy brace around her left arm. She grimaced, slightly, her hand going between her legs.

"You've got a catheter in place," Thayer explained, reading her expression. "I know it's probably not very comfortable."

"That's embarrassing." Corey winced.

"It's necessary. It will be removed as soon as you're stronger."

"You didn't place it, I hope."

Thayer smiled. "I did not. I can remove it when it's time, if you like."

"I think I'll leave it to the professionals." Corey managed a smile. "Peeing through a tube is decidedly not tough."

"Oh, no." Thayer shook her head. "You are absolutely the strongest most courageous person I have ever known."

"Why? What did I do? What happened?"

Thayer realized her mistake. Corey couldn't remember and it was better that way, at least until she was stronger. "Oh, you know." She waved a dismissive hand. "You just never back down from a fight."

Corey's brow furrowed in concentration and she stared at the ceiling. The tightness around her eyes revealed the pain was breaking through. "Please, tell me what happened, Thayer."

"I will. I promise." Thayer kissed the back of her hand. "What you need to worry about now is getting well, okay?"

"Everyone decent?" Collier boomed from outside the door.

Thayer sighed. She didn't have much time with Corey until she had to get to work. "Is it okay?"

"Collier's here?" Corey asked, confused. "Yeah, he can come in." She managed to straighten herself in the bed as much as possible and raked a hand through her hair.

"You look great." Thayer smiled at her.

"Hey, Doc." Collier gave Thayer a nod. "Corey, how you feeling?"

"Corey? Why the hell are you calling me that?" Her eyes widened. "What? Am I dying and no one told me?"

Thayer smothered a laugh and Collier reddened and sighed. "Don't break my balls, Curtis."

"Were you worried about me, Collier? How'd you even know I was here?"

Collier shot a look to Thayer. He pulled a file folder from beneath his arm and tapped it in his hand. "Came by right after you got hurt, but you were getting scanned or some shit. Then you might as well have been dead for the next two days."

"Yeah, well, I'm here now." She offered him a small smile.

"You mind giving us a few minutes, Doc?" he asked Thayer. "I need to get a statement so I can close this case out."

Thayer stiffened, her eyes darting to Corey. "She still has no memory of the fall. Isn't my statement enough?"

"Just being thorough. And yes, we have everything we need. He's talking up a storm but I'd look like a real amateur if I didn't have a record of speaking to one of the victims."

"Victim?" Corey's gaze flicked between them. "Your victim is right here and she can speak for herself."

Thayer blew out a resigned breath and stood. "She doesn't remember and I haven't told her." She gestured helplessly to Jim. "But she deserves to know so it might as well be you."

"Know what? What's going on?"

Thayer gave her hand a final squeeze. "I'm going to make some phone calls." She looked to Jim. "I'll be right outside at the desk."

"Well?" Corey looked sharply at Collier, who was shuffling his feet. "Are you going to tell me or not?"

Collier snapped into professional mode and pulled his notebook from his breast pocket. "Why don't you start with the last thing you remember?"

"Fine." Corey tried to relax back against the pillows. She fiddled with the med pump in her lap but didn't press it despite her growing pain. She needed to think as clearly as possible and her confusion about Thayer's evasiveness over what happened was upsetting her. "Thayer came with me to the memorial for Gordon Akers. I went to return some personal items I still had." She left out the details, unsure what Collier already knew. "We maybe had plans afterward. I don't remember exactly."

"A date?"

"Um, yeah." Corey smiled slightly. "I think so, but before that I wanted to go back to the construction site."

"Back?" Collier's head snapped up, his eyes narrowing.

Corey winced at his glare. "I was there once before. I wanted to get a look at that airshaft. There were inconsistencies in the skull fracture patterns and I—"

"Jesus Christ, Curtis," he sighed.

"What?" She tried to glare back but it just sent fresh pain searing behind her eyes. "There was always something off about Gordon Akers's death and I tried to talk to you…" She swallowed hard and closed her eyes against waves of nausea.

"Are you all right?" He stepped closer. "Do you want me to get—"

"No." Corey's eyes snapped open. "I want someone to tell me what the hell is going on."

"Okay." Collier studied her a moment longer. "Let's start back farther. What happened the first time you went to the site? When was that and was the doc with you?"

"No." Corey worked to breathe evenly. "Cin came with me. We went the day after the post, I think."

"And?" He was scribbling in his notebook. He now had someone else he needed to talk to.

"And we were messing around the shaft at the bottom floor where he was found. I wanted some better pictures, and I wanted to see if there was something there—a ledge, or whatever— that he could have struck on the way down or at the bottom. Something that would have caused the type of fracture to his skull."

"Go on." He was writing furiously.

"There wasn't." She shrugged. "It's smooth all the way down and there was nothing at the bottom. So the ground broke his head apart when he hit, but that didn't explain this long, rounded, depressed fracture we saw that had to happen *before* he hit the ground."

"Did anyone see you there?"

Her brow furrowed in thought. "Yeah, there was this guy there. A worker, I guess. He caught us snooping around. He was a real creep."

"Can you describe him?"

"Um, big, maybe your size, but heavier, fatter. He was pretty unkempt."

He pulled a photo from the folder and handed it to her. "This him?"

She studied the mug shot. The guy's face was pretty banged up but it was clearly the same guy. "Mark Guilford. That's his name? What did he do?"

"Yeah." Collier took the photo back and moved on. "So you went back with the doc to find something that could explain the fracture?"

"Yeah, I think that's right. Maybe? I don't know." She sighed.

He pulled out another photo. "Like this?"

Her hand trembled slightly as she took the picture. It was a length of rebar lying near a pile of rubble. "Where did you find it?"

"I didn't," he corrected. "The doc did. With you." He referred back to his notes. "We had it tested and there's blood on it. It's being run at the lab now to see if the blood matches Gordon Akers's and to see if we can match prints off it, more than just the doc's since she picked it up. Why that idiot didn't just throw it down the refuse chute is anyone's guess."

Corey's head snapped up and she sat straighter in the bed. "Is this a murder weapon? Whose prints? Was I right about his death?"

"Well, you would know better than I if the blow killed him, but if it dented his skull, it probably disabled Akers enough to push or throw him down the airshaft. And that's murder."

"Who?" she asked again. "Who murdered him? That Mark Guilford guy?"

He eyed her. "You really don't remember, do you?"

She looked at him helplessly, feeling the burn of frustrated tears pricking behind her eyes. "No, damn it."

He inhaled deeply and pulled out a stapled sheaf of papers from the folder. "Here."

"What's this?"

"It's the doc's statement about what happened two days ago."

Her trembling increased, from nerves, fear, or pain she didn't know, and she opted to place the sheets on her lap to read them. "Will you raise the lights?"

He looked uncertain. "Are you sure?"

"Yes," she said sharply. "Please turn the lights up."

He did as she asked and she immediately felt the pain ramp up at the bright light, her shaky hand going to the side of her head, but she was determined to read the report.

CHAPTER TWENTY-FOUR

Thayer leaned against the desk at the nurses' station and tapped her foot impatiently. She had already made her calls within her department to set her schedule for the week. Jim was still in with Corey and she was starting to worry about what was taking so long. She was checking her watch again when the door flew open, and Jim, face panicked and eyes darting around, called for her.

"Better get in here, Doc."

Thayer crossed to the room in three strides, sliding by him in the doorway and stopping just inside the door. Corey was pressed back against the bed, eyes screwed shut and her face a mask of pain. Tears streamed down her cheeks and she was breathing in huge gasping sobs.

"Shit."

"Is she having a seizure or something?"

"She's hyperventilating. Can you dim the lights again, please?" Thayer perched on the side of the bed and placed one hand on her chest and the other against her cheek, brushing gently at the tears. "Shh. Shh. Corey, listen to me, honey. You're okay. Just relax and breathe. You're safe now."

Corey's breath shuddered and began to even out at the sound of Thayer's voice, her tension easing. "What were you talking about?" Thayer glanced at the pages, crumpled across Corey's legs.

"She was reading your statement," Collier explained. "Don't think she got very far."

"Oh, damn." Thayer breathed. "Oh, sweetheart, I'm sorry I didn't tell you. You've just been in so much pain I didn't want something else—"

"I'm sor...sorry." Corry hiccupped.

"Shh." Thayer brushed her tears away with her thumb, feeling her heartrate slow beneath her hand. "You're okay. It's okay, now."

"He was there," Corey whispered, her eyes opening to peer at Thayer. "He could have killed you. I didn't know he would be there. I'm so sorry. I didn't know."

"What?" Thayer gaped. "Corey, are you worried you put me in danger?" Fresh tears rolled down her shattered face.

Thayer was speechless, her throat tightening with emotion as she busied herself straightening the papers Corey had been reading. She handed them back to Collier.

"I have what I need for now," he said quietly, taking the pages and leaving without another word.

Thayer picked up the PCA pump and showed Corey she was holding it. "I'm going to push this now, okay?" She waited for Corey to acknowledge her with a small nod. Her agreement confirmed she was hurting. She pressed the button three times.

Corey inhaled deeply, her eyes drifting closed as the meds coursed through her system again.

"Now, I need you to listen to me carefully." Thayer placed her hand against Corey's face and wiped the last of the tears away. "I want you to remember every word I'm about to say."

Corey's normally bright, blue eyes were dull with pain and exhaustion when she opened them again. "I'm listening."

"I am fine. There's not a scratch on me. I am not injured in any way." She spoke slowly and deliberately. Corey's eyes ran the length of her body, narrowing suspiciously. "Okay." Thayer stood and yanked her blouse from her skirt, unbuttoning it from the top. "Remember I believe what comes around goes around." She slipped her arms from the sleeves and stood in front of her in just her bra and skirt so she could see for herself.

Corey's gaze again traveled the length of her, lingering on her breasts. Thayer couldn't help the flush that heated her skin.

She held her arms out and turned around letting her see her back and that she was completely unharmed. "Good?"

Corey blinked slowly, a slow smile coming to her lips. "Yeah."

Thayer fought a smile of her own as she whipped her top back on and hastily buttoned it before dropping back in the chair and gripping Corey's hand. "I know you're fading, honey, but please listen. What you did was so completely selfless and brave I don't even have words."

Corey rolled her eyes. "Nearly getting us killed?"

Thayer sighed. "Well, yes, there were a series of decisions made that, in retrospect, could have been better thought out. But I was there, too, so I share in that responsibility. In our defense we couldn't have known what was going to happen, and I don't think either one of us really believed we were about to uncover a murder."

Thayer gripped her hand hard. "I'm talking about your commitment and passion for your work. Your attention to detail and refusal to believe what everyone else was telling you because you knew something wasn't right. You trusted your instincts and went after what you knew to be true, against the advice of experts. Because of that, a murderer was discovered and justice won. I'm talking about standing up for and speaking up for people who can't do it for themselves. You did that."

Corey was watching her with hooded, glassy eyes, and her breathing slowed. She kissed the back of her hand and held it to her cheek. "I am so impressed by you." She trailed off, her voice hitching as she looked away. "And I promised myself I wouldn't put this out there because it's completely crazy and you have enough to worry about, but maybe it can be something for you to look forward to because it is for me… So, hell, I'm doing it." She looked back and Corey's eyes were closed, her face slack in sleep. Thayer smoothed her hand across her brow. "I'm falling in love with you, Corey Curtis."

With Corey heavily medicated again, Thayer couldn't justify staying, as much as she would have liked to just hold Corey's hand for a little while longer. Simply being with her calmed Thayer in a way she couldn't define.

She was early for her shift and desperately needed a coffee. Dana was right. The nurses made better coffee and she wasn't ready to run into the residents yet, so she settled onto the sofa in the nurses' lounge with her cup and collected herself.

Thayer heard the door bang open and cracked an eye to see Dana hustle in, stopping short when she saw her.

"Hey," she said softly. "Are you coming or going?"

Thayer sat up and tried to look alert. "Coming." She sighed heavily. "Why? Because I look like I just worked a double?"

Dana smiled. "You said it, not me."

"Yeah, I know." She tried to run her fingers through her hair, but they got tangled in snarls she'd failed to brush out earlier. "With any luck I may keep the oglers at bay tonight."

"That's the spirit." Dana dropped onto the sofa next to her and placed a hand on her leg. "How's she doing?"

"Better, I think." Thayer grimaced. "I don't know really. Physically she's improving but she's in a lot of pain, but honestly that's not what worries me most."

"What do you mean?"

"She can't remember what happened and that's a really scary place to be. She heard a lot tonight when Jim Collier came by to take her statement. It was hard. She's confused and feeling guilty, like she endangered me. She's weak and hurting and has no memories to draw from."

"It may come back to her in time."

"Yeah, I know." Thayer was quiet for a moment. "I hope it does. I think it will help her feel more in control."

"That's tough feeling like that. Kind of like Nana, right? The unexpected loss of her independence? A capable woman all of a sudden feeling diminished and reliant on others? It's going to hit her hard."

Thayer turned and stared at her friend. "Yes, that's it exactly. Corey is so physically and mentally strong, and so accomplished. Everything she does and enjoys demands that strength."

"She's going to get angry," Dana said bluntly. "We see it all the time and you know it better than anyone."

Thayer nodded. "I can handle it."

"I know you can." Dana gave her leg a squeeze. "I have to get ready. I'm going to pop up and see her later." She pulled a magazine from her bag. "It's a whole issue of naked athletes in various sporty poses. I don't really get it, but whatever."

Thayer smiled. "She'll love that."

CHAPTER TWENTY-FIVE

If Thayer looked even half as exhausted as she felt, the only looks she would be getting would be ones of fright. She trudged up the stairs to the third floor after her shift.

She had slipped in to see Corey once, but she had been sleeping soundly. It was just after nine a.m. now and the hospital was coming alive with the start of new shifts, visiting hours on all floors and the delivery of breakfast.

She looked up in time to avoid a nurse coming out of Corey's room. Thayer had seen her before a few times and thought her name was Deb. She was an older, no-nonsense woman in her fifties with an unflappable attitude that said she had seen it all. Her bright, warm eyes said she still cared. She was removing the heart rate and oxygen monitors. "Good morning, Dr. Reynolds."

"Good morning." Thayer mustered a smile. "She awake?"

"She is now." Deb snorted a laugh. "Having a catheter yanked will do that."

"Ugh." Thayer sighed. "Well, once she gets over the indignity of it all I'm sure she'll be in a better mood."

"Couldn't be in a worse one," the woman replied.

"Thanks, Deb." Thayer gambled and said her name and was rewarded with a bright smile that said she was pleased someone bothered to learn it.

Corey stared out the window, her face strained and stormy, not acknowledging the opening door. "Here to violate me again?"

"Only if you ask nicely," Thayer teased and moved around to her good side.

She was unhooked from everything but her IV for fluids and meds. Her catheter and chest tube had been removed and her arm now sported a purple cast past her elbow immobilizing her arm at a ninety-degree angle.

"Hey." Corey's mood was dark enough that she didn't reply in kind and her smile looked forced. "Rough night?"

Thayer smiled grimly. "It shows, huh?"

"I'd still trade places with you."

Thayer studied her with a professional eye. She had a little more color today and was more alert but she still had the glassy, heavy-lidded look of someone on pain meds. "You're looking better."

"Better than dead, you mean?"

"Come on, now." Thayer sat and reached for her hand. Corey didn't pull away but she didn't return her grip either. "It's only been a few days. Give yourself a break, Corey. Your injuries are serious and you're not going to get better overnight."

Thayer meant to cheer her but Corey's expression darkened further. Thayer was grateful when there was a knock at the door, thinking it would be someone Corey might be happier to see.

"Good, you're both here." Collier didn't waste time with niceties. "I have to be in court in an hour but I wanted to let you know we've wrapped things up. Mark Guilford has pleaded out to Murder Two for Gordon Akers's death and three counts of assault, two against you, Curtis, and one against the doc. All lesser charges were dropped."

Thayer glanced at Corey, whose face remained stony, her lips in a tight line. "Is that what you were hoping for?"

"He's going away for a long time. All because he got fired."

"What?" Thayer gasped.

Corey's eyes flashed angrily. "Fired?"

"He did two years for a past assault and had long a history of alcohol abuse. Akers took a chance and hired him. They'd worked together in the past on the same crew and Akers was big on second chances."

"Go on." Corey said through gritted teeth. Thayer couldn't tell if it was fury or pain tightening her voice.

"Akers asked him to stay after the other guys left to let him go. Gave him two weeks' notice and severance, which is more than he deserved for shitty work and drinking on the job."

Thayer felt a heaviness in her heart about a good, generous man's unnecessary and violent death. "So, Mark Guilford killed him and tried to cover it up by making it look like he fell while smoking after hours?"

"Seems so. Guilford claims he'd been drinking. Was going to claim diminished capacity, which I believe to an extent because of how stupid he was to throw his own lighter down the shaft and not dispose of the murder weapon. He didn't know Akers had quit smoking. It would have worked, too, if not for all the trouble he caused trying to get it back."

Thayer shook her head in disbelief. "How did he know to go after Corey?"

"Claims he didn't. After finding out from Akers's wife that she didn't have the lighter, he figured it might still be in the morgue. He was parked up the road deciding what to do when he saw Corey drive in. He recognized her from the site when she was out there taking pictures. He followed her in. The brick was in his truck so he just went for it."

"Jesus Christ," Thayer said. "It all just seems like such a waste."

"No shit," Corey hissed and turned to stare back out the window. Her anger and frustration was nearly palpable.

"Listen. There's not going to be a trial but the press knows now. Did my best to keep your names out of it, but you know how it is."

"We appreciate everything you've done, Jim." Thayer smiled. "We'll be okay."

"Speak for yourself," Corey murmured.

"Hey, Curtis." Collier stepped closer to the bed and waited for her gaze to meet his. "I owe you an apology."

"For what?"

"You tried to tell me something wasn't right about this case and I didn't listen. I should have. You've got good instincts. If not for you, Guilford would have gotten away with murder."

"Don't quit your day job, though, right?" Corey laughed humorlessly.

"No, don't," Collier agreed. "You're exceptional at it." He nodded to Thayer. "Let me know if either of you need anything."

"Thank you." Thayer waved him out and turned back to Corey. "Are you all right?"

"Why wouldn't I be?"

"Corey, please talk to me." Thayer gripped her hand. "I haven't known you long but I sure as hell know this anger isn't you."

"The neurologist warned me some people experience personality changes," she countered.

Thayer frowned. "That's not what this is."

Corey met her eyes. "No. I'm sorry. I don't mean to be such a bitch. I'm just so fucking pissed off."

"I understand. I am too. I'm angry a good man is dead and my heart breaks for his family and the grandchild who will never get to know his grandfather. I'm angry you got hurt—more than I can even explain to you. I would give anything to make this better for you. Please, tell me what I can do."

"You should go home and get some rest." Corey sighed and picked up her call button, pressing it. "I need the bathroom."

"I can help you." Thayer stood.

"No. Don't worry about it. Deb will come."

"You rang, your highness?" Deb had apparently been nearby and was leaning in the doorway within a matter of seconds.

"Yeah." Corey pushed herself up in the bed with effort and a groan of pain. "You reap what you sow, Deb. I need to pee."

"Right this way, milady."

Thayer was forced to move to allow Deb in. She tried not to take it personally, but her heart hurt nonetheless at Corey's distance and rejection of her help. "You're right. I need to get home and sleep. I'm back on tonight. Can I come see you before my shift?" She put extra cheer in her voice but in her own head it sounded like she was fighting tears.

"Yeah, sure." Corey grunted, her gaze focused on the bathroom door as Deb took her weight and they shuffled across the room.

Thayer left without another word.

CHAPTER TWENTY-SIX

Corey was determined to get off IV meds by the end of the day. They made her feel sicker and weaker than she already did. She would rather feel unmedicated pain.

She was disgusted with herself and her bad attitude. She had been a total bitch to Thayer and hadn't even mustered the energy to thank Collier for his work on the case. She knew her anger, guilt, and resentment weren't completely unfounded, but she just couldn't unpack it and deal with it yet.

Fortunately, she hadn't had too much time to think about it as a steady stream of visitors kept her mind occupied. Dr. Webster ambled in with a goofy-looking teddy bear holding a mug with a rainbow sticker and a Get Well balloon, clearly from the hospital gift shop. She doubted he knew how funny that mug was, and she knew it would be her new favorite drinking vessel.

He didn't stay long but took the time to assure her that the morgue was being well taken care of; he was enjoying doing some more teaching and the pathology residents were doing a pretty good job on the posts. In a surprising moment of contrition, he admitted he'd never read Corey's email with her concerns about Gordon Akers's injuries and praised her for her work. He had also approved an order for a new Stryker saw.

Cin came in and smuggled her lunch. She still didn't have much of an appetite but picking at a perfectly cooked burger and fries was far preferable to picking at the totally inedible bland chicken and applesauce the hospital served her.

Cin's version on coverage in the morgue was slightly different than Dr. Webster's. Corey cracked up—painfully—hearing about the resident who cut into an incidental ovarian cyst and got a serous fluid shower. She groaned at the one who tried to Y-incision a woman instead of going underneath in a U-incision, thus totally deforming her breasts and enraging the funeral home.

Dana and Jules came together and brought her back issues of Maxim, which she found particularly adorable but had no intention of looking at. They told her hilarious horror stories of the first-year ED residents, who got vomited, bled or shat on during any particular shift. She wanted to ask about Thayer but resisted. It was her own fault Thayer had left so abruptly and she had no right to ask Thayer's friends to talk about her.

By dinnertime she was exhausted and moderately hungry. She had just raised the lid on her tray, uncovering another sad, pale, tasteless hospital meal when Rachel burst in.

"Put that down and back away slowly."

Corey grinned and salivated at the brown paper bag with the Loco Coyote logo on it. She could smell the Mexican food. She didn't even care what was in the bag since she liked everything on the menu.

Rachel grabbed the tray between two fingertips and wheeled it away from Corey like it was venomous, flinging it the last few feet toward the door. It rolled and crashed against the wall and the pudding cup shot onto the floor. "Jesus, that was close."

She perched on the edge of the bed, dug through the bag and handed Corey a chicken and cheese burrito, brimming with rice and beans. "So, talk to me. How you doing?"

Corey slowly unwrapped her burrito one handed and quietly appreciated Rachel's understanding of her need to do things on her own, however awkward. "They're letting me go home on Thursday."

"Fucking, yeah," Rachel cheered around a mouthful of food.

"Conditionally," she added and eyed Rachel over her burrito as she took her first tentative bite.

"Uh-oh." Rachel returned her look. "What does that mean?"

"It means that I need a babysitter for the first few days."

"Ah." Rachel nodded. "Someone to call the meat wagon if you die in your sleep? Who would post you, anyway? Is that like Schrödinger's autopsy?"

Corey laughed. "Something like that." She looked a question at her.

"What?" Rachel's eyes widened and she swallowed her food hard. "Me?"

"Who else?"

"What about your girlfriend? She's a doctor for shit's sake."

"She's not my..." Corey shook her head. "I just need someone I don't have to pretend with."

Rachel paused. "I can do it, Cor, if that's what you want."

"Thank you." Corey stared at her food.

"When's the last time you had some Coyote?"

"Um, I don't know. Maybe with you?" Her eyes started to lose focus, the room wavering. She closed her eyes for a moment to clear her vision.

"You all right?"

"Yeah. Just something weird with my eyes for a second."

"Thayer been to see you today?"

"This morning." Corey winced. "I wasn't in a very good mood and I was kind of an asshole to her."

"Well, I'm sure, under the circumstances, she'll cut you some slack."

"Yeah, I hope so, because—" Corey winced and stared at Rachel. "I was going to take her to dinner."

"What?"

"Thayer didn't want to go to the construction site." Corey frowned, her hand going to the back of her neck to massage against the pain and tightening muscles. "She wanted to go for Mexican. I said I would take her after we stopped at the site. She didn't want to go in but I insisted. I told her she could wait in the car and she got offended."

"Did someone tell you this or are you remembering?"

"Re...remem...ber..." Corey stammered, her head splitting in sudden pain so sharp her vision blacked out completely. "Oh...God..." She pressed the heel of her hand against the side of her head.

Rachel leapt up and swept away their food. "Corey?"

"Call...Call...the nurse..."

Rachel lunged for the call button and jammed her thumb down on it as Corey groaned in pain, her eyes screwed tightly shut.

"I'm about to go off shift," Deb called from the hallway as she strode in. "What's the problem, princess?"

"Do something," Rachel pleaded.

Deb's expression sobered as she crossed to Corey's side. "Okay, kiddo, here we go." She got a hand behind Corey and encouraged her to sit up. "Post-concussion syndrome, remember? Headaches, dizziness, nausea, blurred vision. Looks like you're covering all the bases."

Corey whimpered pitifully "Sick..."

Deb turned to Rachel. "There's a tub in the bathroom. Get it."

Rachel retrieved the bucket, sliding it in front of Corey a split second before she violently vomited her dinner.

"Her orders are already in for this. We've been expecting it. Are you all right to stay with her while I draw up her meds?"

"Yeah. Yeah, I got her."

"Good girl."

Thayer could hear the sounds of someone's agony as soon as she stepped onto the floor and she winced in sympathy at the unmistakable sound of retching. She realized a moment later it was coming from Corey's room. She hurried to the door, flinging it open to see Corey huddled in her bed vomiting into the plastic tub Rachel held for her.

Rachel looked her way with relief. "Cor, Thayer's here."

"No...no." Corey sobbed around her heaving stomach. "Not...now..."

Thayer's heart broke for her pain and that she could do nothing. "Corey, let me help."

"No." Corey choked, her arm jerking out to wave her away. "Out..."

Thayer stiffened in surprise, her eyes burning with emotion. "Corey."

"Excuse me, Dr. Reynolds." Deb hurried back in, squeezing by Thayer and over to Corey's side. "Corey, you're going to feel better soon, I promise. This is an antinausea med that will settle your stomach." She injected the first syringe into her IV port. "This one is a muscle relaxant to ease the muscle spasms and pain." She injected the second. "They both have strong sedative properties so you're going to feel really drowsy right away."

"Thank you." She breathed and sank back against the bed.

Thayer could see her now, bathed in sweat and gulping breaths but beginning to relax.

Rachel pulled the bowl away, racing to the bathroom to empty it, looking like she might need it herself any minute.

"Is that her first one?" Thayer brought up her professional side to mask her hurt and concern.

"Yes." Deb took her pulse and blood pressure before turning to the compact laptop next to her bed and entering her vitals and updating her chart with medications administered. "We've been expecting it. Dr. Bryant already has a call in for a follow-up CT so we'll see if we can get her in tonight. If everything is still clear, no clots and no swelling, she should still be able to be released the day after tomorrow."

"Released. That's good." Thayer pressed her lips together. "She didn't mention."

"She's going to fall asleep soon. I'll call CT now and get her in tonight, but I should've clocked out a half hour ago. Overtime is met with swift and unpleasant action. I'll get the night nurse to clean her up."

"It's okay." Thayer stepped into the room now. "I have time before I'm on. I'll do it."

Deb looked at her, surprised. "You don't have to do that."

"I know," Thayer said simply.

"Well, okay, then. I'll leave you to it."

Thayer stood next to the bed. Corey's chest rose and fell, haltingly, suggesting she was still uncomfortable, but her face relaxed and her eyes closed to slits. "Hey, sweetheart." Thayer brushed damp hair from her clammy face and thumbed away tears still tracking down her cheeks. "Can you hear me?"

Corey's eyes dragged open. "Thayer..." It was barely a whisper.

"Yes, I'm here."

CHAPTER TWENTY-SEVEN

Corey had been in the chair in her room for over an hour staring at the small container of valium tablets. She had resisted taking them but she desperately needed one to control the headache and muscle spasms in her neck that threatened to overwhelm her. Five days in the hospital and her mood had deteriorated. She had lost weight and despite visits from Cin, Rachel, Jules and constant attention from Thayer when she had slow shifts, she was miserable.

She was being released tomorrow and as much as she looked forward to it, the inevitable conversation with Thayer was weighing heavily on her mind.

She finally could stand it no longer and struggled to her feet. She swallowed the meds with a glass of water and eased herself back into bed. As if she conjured Thayer with her thoughts, there was a soft knock and Thayer let herself in.

"Hey, tough girl."

"Please, stop calling me that," Corey grumbled.

Thayer answered her with a dazzling smile, clearly not letting Corey's foul mood bring her down. "I know you're getting out tomorrow but these were coming up in my yard and I thought you would enjoy them." She placed a vase with a fresh bouquet of wildflowers by the window before settling in the chair Corey had just vacated. "How are you feeling?"

"How do I look?" She shrugged.

"So, I've been thinking about your recovery and I'm sure you have as well. You're going to need some help for a bit and I've talked to my director and he's willing to shuffle my schedule around so I can be home at the critical times—morning and night. I've been meaning to get a television and we can pick up your movies and get started on some. And I can get the fishing gear out so you're not bored—"

"Thayer, wait." Corey sucked in a deep breath, fighting the pull of the medication.

"I have plenty of room and I'll be gone a lot so you won't feel babied, but I'll be around if you need—"

"Thayer, stop," she said more forcefully.

Thayer paused and looked at her. "I know it's overwhelming right now but you're strong and will be back to your old self—"

"It's not a good idea."

"What's not?"

Corey inhaled deeply. "My going home with you."

"Okay. Why not?"

Corey was really regretting those meds as all her carefully planned words were lost to her. She forced a smile. "You know, you take care of people all day and you don't want to come home or wake up to that."

Thayer laughed. "That's absurd. This isn't the same thing at all." She reached for Corey's hand but Corey pulled away and her smile faltered. "What is this about, really?"

Corey looked past her to stare out the window. "Not very heroic of me is it?"

"What?" Thayer's eyes narrowed. "What does that mean?"

"Nothing." Corey shook her head, not meaning to say that out loud. "Never mind."

Thayer scooted to the end of the chair. "Corey, I care about you. A lot. I want to help and I can. Please, don't shut me out."

The meds were taking hold and Corey could feel her emotional walls slipping. She was too tired for evasion. "I don't want you to see me like this."

Thayer jerked in surprise. "Like what? Strong? A fighter? Corey, what you did—"

"I can't remember." Corey could feel her eyes beginning to burn with unshed tears. "I can't remember what I did."

"Then you'll just have to trust me." Thayer smiled gently. "You were amazing."

"And now I'm sick and weak. I can barely wipe my own ass. I have headaches so bad I can't see and then I vomit on myself. And if not, then I'm drugged out of my mind and can't string two words together." She raged, tears beginning to fall. "You don't want any part of that."

Thayer's mouth gaped. "Corey, I don't care—"

"But I do, Thayer. It wasn't supposed to be like this. I'm sorry."

Thayer's expression was stunned "Okay. What do you need?"

"Time." Corey couldn't look at her. She knew she was hurting her and the pain in her heart nearly eclipsed the pain in her head. "Space."

Thayer was quiet a long time then stood. "If that's what you want. I'll back off." Her voice cracked. "Take care of yourself, Corey."

Thayer swiped at the tears on her face as she burst through the door.

Rachel pushed herself off the wall where she had been hovering outside the door. "Thayer."

"Hey, Rachel." Thayer turned and mustered a smile but the look on Rachel's face told her she had heard everything.

"I'm sorry." Rachel's face was pained. "I'll talk to her."

"It's fine." Thayer forced a laugh. "She's scared and feeling vulnerable. Not the foundation you want to build a relationship on. I get it."

"Please, don't give up on her." Rachel's eyes glistened. "She's worth it."

Thayer sobbed a breath, wiping at her eyes again. "I know." She whispered and smiled sadly. "You'll take care of her?"

"Always." Rachel returned her smile. "And knock some sense into her."

Thayer nodded. "I have to get back to work."

"I'll be in touch."

"Thank you." Thayer gripped her arm briefly and was gone.

Corey stared hopefully at the door when it opened again. Her face fell when she saw Rachel.

"She's gone. Just like you asked."

Corey tore her gaze away and stared out the window again.

Rachel sat down. "You okay?"

Corey simply nodded, her eyes growing heavy from the sedative.

Rachel considered a moment. "She's falling in love with you."

Corey's eyes snapped to hers. "What?"

Rachel shrugged. "You heard me."

Corey frowned and shifted on the bed. "Not with this me."

"With every you, you fucking idiot." Rachel pinned her with a look. "I can't even believe I, who has never had a relationship longer than two months, have to explain this to you. Corey, what I said last week about why people want to be with you, be around you, that quality you have is in no way lessened by this. If anything it's heightened. You are a fucking rock star. You should hear how the girls talk about—"

"Don't. Just stop."

"Seriously, you'd think you were dying or something. You broke your arm, busted a few ribs and banged your head. It's a fender bender. It's a rugby match. Fighters suffer worse in the ring."

"Fuck you, Rachel."

"Jesus Christ." Rachel sighed. "You really are feeling sorry for yourself, aren't you?"

"What do you want from me?"

"Who gives a shit what I want?" Rachel stood. "It's what you want that matters. To get better? To get back in shape? To beat me again? To get back to work? To get the girl? Name me one hero who doesn't have someone looking out for them? Pepper Potts, Peggy Carter, Lois Lane, Gwen Stacey. I could go on. And I might add, they are all amazing, beautiful, accomplished women in their own right and *Agent Carter* should never have been canceled, by the way."

"That makes no sense, Rachel." She rolled heavy-lidded eyes to her. "I'm not Iron Man."

"Well, okay," Rachel conceded with a grin. "But he is a deeply flawed, selfish asshole, too."

Corey blinked sluggishly as her words registered and her mouth quirked into the beginnings of a smile. "You're an asshole."

"And proud of it," Rachel said and then grew serious. "Thayer is a spectacular woman. The real deal, although possibly out of her mind because she wants you. Is this really how you want things to go?"

Corey's tears flowed freely now, her heart aching. "I can't have the most intimate moment we've shared be her cleaning up after me, helping me get dressed, or wiping up my puke. Our first shower together isn't supposed to be because I can't wash my own hair. I can't do it, Rachel. I won't."

"Okay, Corey." Rachel nodded. "I get it. I do."

"Will you just take me home tomorrow, please?" Her eyes drooped.

"I'll be here."

CHAPTER TWENTY-EIGHT

"Jesus, finally." Corey eased herself off the bed when Rachel banged back into the room with the wheelchair. "What took so fucking long?"

Rachel had shown up just after noon with clothes and shoes for her and disappeared to the main desk to go over Corey's instructions, pick up her meds, and get her discharged. It was now after three and Rachel looked just as annoyed as Corey felt. The most exciting thing that had happened to her all morning was Deb coming in to remove the sutures from the back of her head, the ones Thayer had put in a lifetime ago.

"Don't even start," Rachel grumbled. "I think it would have been easier to break you out of jail than what I just went through. The paperwork was ridiculous and then I had to wait at the pharmacy and then—you know what—I don't even want to relive it." She backed the wheelchair up and put the brakes on. She helped herself to water off the bedside table while Corey lowered herself into the chair. "You have everything?"

Corey had a plastic bag with the Get Well cards and the rainbow mug in her lap. The magazines had already been redistributed to the other patients on the floor. Her gaze lingered on the flowers Thayer had brought her, which looked lovely in the afternoon sun. Corey's heart lurched, imagining Thayer carefully choosing each one just for her. "Yeah, I have everything."

"All right. Let's roll." Rachel grinned, released the brakes and immediately crashed Corey into the doorframe. "Shit."

"Come on, man," Corey grunted as her sore ribs jarred.

"Sorry. Sorry."

Thayer had a pretty good view of the main hospital entrance from the ED ambulance bay as she leaned in the doorway and watched Rachel push Corey out to the parking lot from a hundred yards away. It was like Corey had taken a restraining order out on her, and she was absolutely not going to violate it.

"Brought you a good coffee." Dana held out a fresh cup.

"Thank you." Thayer took it, her eyes never leaving the parking lot.

Dana followed her gaze. "You didn't want to be there?"

"She didn't want me there." Thayer sighed. "Or anywhere, I guess."

"What do you mean?"

"Time and space." Thayer shrugged. "She wants me to back off, so I am. I did."

"She doesn't really want that. You know that, right?"

"Maybe, but she's going to have to figure that out on her own. She knows how to find me and I'm not going anywhere." Thayer took a sip of her coffee. "But I'm not going to crowd her."

"How long are you going to wait?"

Thayer laughed. "I'm not looking for another relationship. I wasn't looking for a relationship with her. Well, I guess I did literally go looking for her, but I had no idea what was going to happen—if you can even call it a relationship. I don't even think we got that far. I've got my job and the house and Nana to visit. I'm going to be fine."

"Doesn't make it hurt less, though." Dana placed a hand on her arm.

"No." Thayer sucked in a breath. "No, it doesn't."

"So, I guess that explains why your name is on the board for every other shift."

Thayer smiled thinly. "Working helps keep me from getting stuck in my head wondering what I could have done differently. It's silly, I know. I mean we hardly know each other. I just thought…" She studied her coffee.

"You thought right," Dana said firmly. "I could see it and she will too. And if she doesn't, she's a damn fool. And Corey Curtis may be a lot of things, but a fool, she is not."

Thayer smiled genuinely at her. "Thanks, Dana. You're a good friend."

"I know. Now, get back to work." She thrust a chart at her. "There's a sixteen-year-old girl obviously close to term, complaining of back and abdominal pain and her mother is insisting she's never had sex."

Thayer rolled her eyes and took the chart, handing Dana her coffee. "Another virgin birth. Hallelujah."

Rachel pulled her car in behind Corey's truck and parked.

"Thanks for getting my truck back."

"Wasn't me." Rachel grabbed the bag of her stuff and got out coming around to the passenger side.

"Thayer." Corey sighed as she stepped slowly out of the car and stood, wobbling for a moment, until she could straighten and gain her balance.

"Actually, I'm pretty sure Thayer rode with you in the ambulance. I think Sergeant Collier had an officer drive it back after they collected the evidence they needed."

Corey thought about that as they made their way slowly into her place. Thayer holding her hand, bossing around the paramedics. She was sexy as hell when she was being professional. She couldn't help the smile that snuck up on her. She cleared her throat. "Right. Sergeant Collier. I haven't had the chance to ask you about that."

Rachel groaned theatrically as she let them in. "I was hoping that was part of your memory loss." She dropped the bag and Corey's keys on the counter. "I'll tell you over dinner, but it's not really table talk. Are you hungry?"

It hadn't occurred to her that she was hungry until she noticed how wonderful her condo smelled. Lasagna and garlic bread if she was right. "Did you make snacks, you big softie? I didn't even know you cooked."

"I don't." Rachel walked with her to the dining table. "This one is all Thayer. Her grandmother's recipe I think she said. Hang on and I'll get you a plate."

Corey sank painfully onto a chair, the weight of her heart pressing her down. Thayer stayed away, respecting her request for space. She had far too much class and self-respect to do otherwise, but she wasn't going to pretend she didn't care so she had made her dinner for her first day home. Corey wanted to laugh and cry simultaneously. "Thanks," she managed as Rachel set a steaming plate of lasagna before her.

"I hope you don't think I'm not going to drink because you can't." Rachel returned with a beer for herself and water for Corey.

"Never crossed my mind."

She stared at her plate of meaty lasagna with melty cheese and wondered how much time Thayer had spent making it. Corey wasn't much of a cook herself but she loved to barbecue, especially in the summer. Her brain went off the rails to images of Thayer, a glass of wine in her hand, relaxing on her back deck while Corey grilled steaks. They laughed as they shared stories from college and places they'd traveled.

"You can call her, you know. Let her know you're home." Rachel wasted no time diving into her food. "You have the technology and I know she would like to hear from you."

Corey snapped back to reality. "And you know that because you've spoken with her recently?"

Rachel took a long pull of her beer, looking at her over her bottle. "Yes."

Corey nodded and started on dinner. "Thought so." It was delicious and the most she had eaten since the accident. "Tell me about Collier."

"Shit." Rachel grimaced and ate a few more bites before finishing her beer. She got up and got another one before starting her story. "You met his son Andrew?"

"Once or twice."

"We were in JCU together as freshmen before I dropped out. Before you moved back here." She paused and worked on her beer.

Corey's drug-addled mind wasn't that addled. "You and Andrew?"

"You've seen him," Rachel answered as if that explained everything.

"Yeah, he is a good-looking guy." Corey grinned. "What happened?"

"Nothing." Rachel shrugged. "We were dating, having fun, you know. He had a place off campus and I was there when his father showed up unannounced one night with surprise hockey tickets. Well, he had a key and let himself in."

"Oh, shit. What did you do?"

"Swallowed fast." Rachel raised her bottle with a smirk.

Corey blinked at her before her words registered and she started to laugh, gripping her side. "What did Collier do?"

"Well, he didn't arrest me for blowing his son if that's what you're thinking, but if you've ever looked up the word awkward I'm pretty sure that image is there."

CHAPTER TWENTY-NINE

Corey's happy homecoming was short-lived as she was wrenched violently from her first night in her own bed. She stumbled to the bathroom, vomited her dinner, and collapsed in the bathroom from a brutal, disabling headache until Rachel could get her meds into her and Corey could keep them down. Rachel held her on the tile floor while Corey shook and cried from the pain until she calmed enough to be helped back to bed, finally finding peace with heavily sedated sleep.

Her physical health should have been improving, but her mental state deteriorated rapidly, leaving her listless and dispirited. Despite Rachel's herculean efforts to engage and enliven her with offers to go out, go to the gym, or simply take a walk around the neighborhood, Corey continued to spiral down.

"Hi, honey, I'm home," Rachel called as she dropped her keys on the bar. She stopped short when she saw Corey sacked out on the sofa. "Jesus Christ, have you even moved, today? Or, yesterday? When is the last time you took a shower?" She glared at the television. "You haven't even changed the movie." She sighed, her gaze scanning the apartment. "What the fuck, Corey?"

Corey dragged dull, drowsy eyes to her. "What?"

Rachel shook her head as she perched on the armchair. "When you said you wanted someone you didn't have to pretend with, and you pushed Thayer away because you didn't want her to see you like this, I thought you meant you didn't want her to see you struggle or be in pain. Not when you were just getting to know each other and just starting your courtship. I totally got that. And, by the way, she did too, and she's waiting patiently for you to get it together because I told her you were worth it."

Corey glared at her, her throat tightening at the reminder of how she had hurt Thayer. "What's your point?"

"My point," Rachel stood and swiped at a stack of takeout cartons, scattering them across the floor, "is that I'm not your fucking nursemaid. I came here to help you get well, not enable you to wallow in your own filth and self-pity. I get that you're tired and hurting and pissed off, but this is not who you are. There are things you could be doing to help with the headaches, and it just so happens one of those things is stretching and exercise, something I know you enjoy."

"Get real, Rachel."

"All right," Rachel said bitterly. "How's this for real? I'm going home for a couple hours. I told the girls I'd work with them on their takedowns tonight. You know, the girls who think you walk on water? I'm going to stop back by here on my way over to the gym. If nothing has changed, I swear to Christ, Corey, I love you, you know I do, but I'm not coming back. This is bullshit, and you fucking well know it."

Corey struggled to sit up, her eyes widening at Rachel's tongue-lashing. "Wait—"

"And on my way out I'm going to call Thayer and tell her to move on. That I was wrong and she could do better than wasting her time on a selfish piece of shit like Corey Curtis." She snatched her keys from the bar. "Fucking real enough for you?" she yelled as she slammed the door.

Corey sat on the edge of the sofa and ran her hand through her greasy hair. "Fuck." She trembled slightly at Rachel's rage while her words still reverberated around the room and through her head, every single one of them a sharp strike to what was left of her pride and self-respect.

Her jaw clenched and unclenched in anger, not at Rachel but at herself, as she pushed herself to her feet and went in search of a trash bag before she turned off the television and put on some music.

By the time she was finished picking up and cleaning, she was drenched in sweat, her ribs aching mercilessly, but she was determined to be ready when Rachel returned. She had disgraced herself and their friendship, and she would never forgive herself if she didn't make things right.

She navigated the shower, her cast wrapped in plastic and sticking out the curtain while she washed her hair twice. She struggled into jeans for the first time and pulled a T-shirt over her head, threading her cast through the sleeve.

She hadn't heard Rachel come back and was startled to see her as she limped her way back downstairs, her sneakers in her right hand, her cast tucked up against her ribs. "Hey."

Rachel looked around the tidy living room and kitchen before meeting Corey's gaze. "I'm sorry."

She winced as she lowered herself onto the sofa and dropped her sneakers in front of her, aiming her feet into them without bending over. "No, you're not."

Rachel nodded and crouched in front of her, helping her into her shoes and lacing them up. "No, I'm not." She sat back on her heels and looked at her friend, her pain obvious. "I'll get you something for the pain."

"No." Corey wanted to be free of the drugs. "I'll be all right."

"Don't, Corey," Rachel scolded as she rose. "I made my point and you heard me. It's true, you don't have to pretend with me, okay?"

"Okay." Corey managed a smile and took the tablets Rachel handed her with a bottle of water.

"Where are you going anyway?" Rachel asked.

"With you."

"Holy shit, it's Corey." The blonde nudged the brunette.

"Corey, you're back," the brunette exclaimed as she caught sight of the two of them.

"Which one is which?" Corey murmured through her smile as they made their way toward the ring. On her best day she had to struggle to remember who was Emily and who was Emma.

"Emma is the cute one," Rachel replied under her breath.

Her gaze darted between them—both small, fit, and the kind of adorable only college-age girls with names like Emily and Emma could be. "You're a bitch and I hate you," Corey hissed.

Rachel laughed as they approached. "Hey, Emily, hey, Emma," she greeted them, clearly indicating who was who and gave Corey a wink.

"Corey, oh, my god, how are you?" Emily, the blonde, gripped Corey's good arm. "When did you get out of the hospital?"

"I'm better, Emily, thank you." Corey smiled at her. "I've been out a few days."

"When are you getting back in the ring?" Emma asked. "Guess it will be a while yet, huh?" She smoothed a hand over Corey's cast in a flirty gesture.

"Um…" Corey swallowed. "Yeah, it was a clean break but still five more weeks."

"Oh, no one has signed it yet." Emma noticed, her eyes lighting up. "Can I be the first? There's a marker in the equipment room." She ran off without waiting for an answer.

"Come on, Emily." Rachel nodded toward the ring. "Let's get started."

Corey wandered around the gym, greeting the other women she knew and meeting some women she didn't, talking a bit about the case since it was public knowledge, and answering questions about her injuries and recovery. She had to admit it was good to be back and she felt better, stronger, and more at peace just being here. She wouldn't have ever guessed how much her gym community was a part of her identity until she was denied it for so long.

She brushed her fingertips across the free weights, passing over the twenty-five-pound weight she would normally curl and picking up a fifteen. She sat on the bench and managed ten repetitions with her right arm before her protesting ribs could no longer be ignored. Still, it was a start and she planned to come back in the morning. At the heavy bag, Emma caught up with her.

"Found it." She held up a black permanent marker and grinned mischievously. "May I?"

"Oh, yeah, sure." Corey held her arm out as best she could. She tried to see what Emma was writing, since it took a really long time, but the young woman was careful to block Corey's line of sight.

"Done." Emma grinned, her eyes flashing brightly. "What do you think?"

Corey looked down. She had drawn a surprisingly well-crafted image of kissing lips and little hearts so Corey could see it. Next to it she had written something about kissing it better and then her name. Corey jerked her gaze away. "Uh, you're a pretty good artist."

"I'm pretty good at a lot of things." Emma smiled seductively, her intentions clear. "You're right-handed, correct?"

"I, uh, yes," Corey stammered and held up her hand. "I am, yes. Actually, I was going to try throwing a few punches. Do you mind holding the bag for me?" It wasn't altogether a lie and the first thing that popped into her head to distract Emma.

"Sure." Emma stepped behind the bag, holding it with her arms and body and peering around the side. "I'm ready whenever you are, Corey."

Corey cleared her throat and pretended she didn't understand the double meaning. "Thanks." She moved into a modified fighting stance, left leg forward and left arm up as much as the cast would allow, and right hand fisted at the ready. She moved slowly, twisting her body with careful deliberation as she exhaled and her right fist made contact with the bag. A flash of pain through her chest had her canting to the left until it passed.

"Are you all right?" Emma eyed her with real concern. "Maybe you shouldn't—"

"No. It's fine." Corey was determined now. It hurt but felt good to work her body again.

She put a little bounce into her stance and got her arms up again. She hit the bag with more force, putting some weight behind it. Her vision wavered and she swayed with pain as the image of Mark Guilford coalesced in her mind—on his knees, a hand grabbing at his crotch as he tried to rise. She put everything she had behind that swing and he went down. She saw Thayer trapped on the scaffolding, watching her with frantic eyes and then relief as he went down and was still. She smiled at Thayer and then felt her stomach drop.

"Corey!"

She couldn't tell who the voice belonged to and she felt an arm go around her waist and move her, hands guiding her to sit on something hard. A bench at the gym.

"Rachel," Emma yelled.

She sucked in deep breaths, her muscles spasming and her stomach turning over but settling after a moment. She massaged the back of her neck. "I'm okay."

"Hey, Cor, what's going on?" Rachel was there, kneeling in front of her. A few of the other women stood nearby.

"I'm okay." She exhaled, keeping her eyes closed. "I just remembered something from the accident and it overwhelmed me, I think."

"Are you getting a headache?" Rachel asked with concern.

"No. I don't know. Maybe." She cracked her eyes. She squinted against the light. Her pain didn't get worse, but it didn't get better either.

"We should go." Rachel started pulling off her gloves.

"No." Corey covered her hands with her own. "This isn't going to control my life."

"Corey—"

"I'm okay, Rachel," Corey insisted. "I'll just sit. Finish your training."

Rachel considered. "Are you sure? Because I'm the one who's going to have to clean it up if your head explodes."

"I'm sure." Corey smiled. "I need to deal. I'll be okay."

Rachel grinned. "Atta girl."

CHAPTER THIRTY

Each day Corey waited until the morning rush was over at the gym. She didn't want to be in anyone's way, attract a lot of attention, or struggle in front of too many people. She was limited in what she could do still, but she made use of the free weights and all the leg machines and spent a lot of time stretching. It was exhausting and painful and Corey was determined to get it done every morning before she did anything else. Her stubbornness was rewarded with daily improvement, which made the next day that much easier.

After only a week she noticed a difference in the intensity of her pain. She was on the right track and intended to call the physical therapy department and make her first appointment, which was what she was thinking about when she nearly hit the car parked in front of her condo.

She eyed it through the windshield, a silver metallic Toyota Camry hybrid—Anna's car. She hadn't seen or spoken to her ex since she'd stood Anna and her parents up for dinner and now she was sitting on her front step. Anna looked up from her phone as Corey got out of her truck.

"Hi." Anna slipped her phone into her briefcase and stood, brushing off the slacks of her suit.

"Hi." Corey studied her. She looked exactly the same—cool, beautiful, and serious. Her straight, dark hair pinned up in the back and her suit expertly tailored.

Anna looked her over. "You look better than I expected."

"Um, thanks, I guess."

"That didn't come out right." Anna smiled. "How are you?"

"Better than I expected." Corey offered with a smile. "Did you want to come in?"

Anna glanced at the front door, considering. "I don't think so. I still have a few minutes, though." She gestured to the front step and resumed her seat.

"Yeah, sure." Corey eased next to her, unable to totally stifle a grunt of pain.

"Are you all right?"

"I'm fine," she assured her. "Just a little sore."

Anna took a deep breath. "I saw what happened on the news. I couldn't believe it when they started talking about you. I had a few people over at the time and I dropped my wineglass when your name came up, shattering it all over the floor. Like you see in the movies."

She laughed. "Sorry to ruin your dinner party."

"No, that's not what I meant." Anna sighed. "I was worried about you. No matter what happened between us, Corey, I do care about you."

Corey winced. "Anna, I'm sorry about—"

"I didn't come here for an apology. I'm not angry anymore. It was never right with us and I knew it too. I could have called it anytime, but I didn't."

"Okay. How are you?"

"Seeing someone, actually." Anna's face brightened. "She's been right in front of me for a long time."

"Yeah?" Corey grinned. "That's great. Anyone I know?"

"Um, Megan from my office."

"Megan, your secretary? You're sleeping with your secretary?"

"Administrative Assistant," Anna corrected. "And she got promoted, so stop judging." Anna tried not to smile.

"Oh, okay, then."

"What about you? I saw a picture of your doctor friend on the news. The one that was there with you." Anna whistled in appreciation. "What's going on there?"

"Oh, uh…" Corey sucked in a breath. "It's complicated."

"She married?"

"What? No."

"Straight?"

"No."

"You don't find her attractive?" Anna suggested, mockingly.

"Come on." She didn't want to be teased about Thayer.

"Then what's complicated about it?"

Corey stared at the ground and massaged the back of her neck, absently. "Me, I guess." She finally looked back up. "I complicated it."

"For a good reason, I'm sure."

"Pride? Vanity? Self-absorption?" Corey shrugged. "Pick one."

"About the shittiest reasons there are. Can you fix it?"

Corey paused. "I think so, yes."

"Do you want to?"

Corey's throat closed, tears threatening as she thought of how badly she missed Thayer, how empty her bed felt, though they hadn't yet done more than kiss and hold hands. How badly she missed her laugh and the way her golden eyes sparkled when Thayer looked at her right before she teased her. All she could do was nod.

"Oh, wow." Anna smiled, sympathetically. "It's her, isn't it? She's the one?"

"How could I possibly know that?"

"How long have you known her?"

"Oh, um, we just met right around the time you and I ended, I guess."

Anna did some mental math. "So, three weeks?"

"Well, I haven't seen her since I've been out of the hospital, and I was in the hospital for a week and not really able to… Well, let's say I've had better days."

"So…" Anna wrote imaginary numbers in the air and stuck her tongue out comically like she was concentrating. "…carry the two…one week. That sound right?"

Corey blew out a breath. "Is that all? God, it feels like I've known her forever."

Anna smiled, knowingly. "And that, my friend, is your answer." She gave her leg a gentle squeeze and rose to her feet before extending her hand and helping Corey to hers. "Now I'm late for a client meeting."

"Thank you for coming by. It means a lot."

"Can I give you a hug?" Corey raised her right arm and invited her closer, Anna wrapped her arms around her gently. "I'm really glad you're okay."

"Thanks. I'm glad you're happy with Megan."

Anna stepped back and gave Corey a stern look. "I meant what I said. When you find her, treat her better. Got it?"

"Yes, ma'am."

Thayer linked her arm through her grandmother's as they started on the familiar path that ran around the small pond at her assisted living home. She didn't the need the help. She was small and she shuffled slightly from the partial paralysis, but she was still the most capable woman Thayer knew.

Whenever Thayer wasn't working these days, she was sleeping or nurturing the relationships in her life she could still protect. "Do you want to go all the way around today?"

"It's only half a mile," her grandmother scoffed. "Why? Are you going to have trouble?"

Thayer laughed. "I was just asking."

They were quiet for several minutes as they picked their way over some roots at the start of the path. "You haven't been around much the last couple of weeks, Jo." Her grandmother, while honored at her daughter's name choice for her only child, had felt it silly to call her granddaughter by her own last name so she used her middle name, Josephine. "Is everything all right?"

"I know, I'm sorry Nana. I've been working a lot."

"And spending time with that strapping young woman, Corey, I hope. When are you going to bring her by so I can meet her?"

"Strapping?"

"Is that not how you would describe her?"

"It works, I guess." Thayer cleared her throat. "But no, we haven't seen much of each other since she got hurt."

"Oh, my, she's not still in the hospital is she?"

"No, nothing like that." Thayer considered her words carefully. "She just wanted to prioritize her recovery over starting a relationship."

"Hmm." Nana was quiet a long time. "And what did you want?"

"I guess I thought we would heal together."

"Did you tell her that?"

"I did. I mean, I think I did. She was sensitive and self-conscious about being hurt and needing to rely on other people. She was angry."

"Well, I wouldn't know anything about that now, would I?" Nana chuckled and squeezed her arm.

"I told her that didn't matter to me. She was still the same woman I fell…that I, um… I let her know I wanted to help but she didn't want it. Not from me."

"Did you tell her you needed her help too?"

"What do you mean?"

"I mean when you're overwhelmed and scared and feeling like you can't do the things you used to do, it's nice to hear—you need to hear—how valued you are. That someone needs a thing only you can provide. That's why, since I moved in here, we now have a beautiful butterfly garden." Nana paused and stared out over the pond to watch a heron fishing for lunch. "Maybe you can tell her that."

Thayer swallowed hard. "She doesn't want to talk to me."

"Now, I'm certain that's not true."
"How are you so sure?"
"Because you're a real dish, Jo."

CHAPTER THIRTY-ONE

Corey looked up and watched as Rachel banged open the front door of her condo and tore through the entryway into the living room. She had quit staying over shortly after Corey's first trip back to the gym but held on to a key in case of emergency. There had been two since, both on days after Corey had grossly overexerted herself, once physically and once emotionally, in her quest to get back in shape and get healthy.

With her return to the gym came her resolve to heal in mind and body. She worked out daily, and her increased strength decreased her headaches and need for medication.

"Corey!"

"I'm right here." She leaned on the kitchen counter.

Rachel moved into the kitchen and stopped when she saw Corey packing up a cooler and dropping items into a shopping bag. "What? What the hell? Are you all right?"

Corey straightened. "Yeah, fine." She grinned. "Can you help me load up my truck?"

Rachel gaped at her. "Shit, Cor, I thought you were dying."

"What? Why? All I said was could you come over and help me."

"ASAP," Rachel yelled. "Come over ASAP."

"Shit. Sorry." Corey grimaced. "I was running short on time and I didn't realize how that would sound."

"Christ." Rachel ran her hands through her hair, standing it on end. "I have a date, Corey."

"You do? Who with?"

"This guy, Jude." Rachel's face softened. "He's been coming into the shop the last week or so. I thought he was a real creeper at first, but he's got the cutest dimple so I could hit that."

"Yeah?" She fought a laugh. "What's his deal?"

"Don't know yet but I've seen him pull up in a hearse and that's kind of rad." Rachel's brow furrowed. "Wait, do you know him?"

She grinned. "He's a good guy."

"I feel like sex in a hearse is something I should—"

"Dude, no." She shook her head.

"Yeah, you're right." Rachel still seemed to be thinking about it as she hefted the cooler. "What the fuck is in this?" She grunted as Corey raced around her and got the door.

"Dinner for two." Corey ran back and grabbed the shopping bags.

Rachel paused on the walkway. "You called Thayer?"

"Not exactly." She set the bags on the passenger seat of her truck and ran around to lower the tailgate.

"Texted?" Rachel grunted as she heaved the cooler into the back and slid it in.

"Um, no."

"What then?"

"A surprise?"

Rachel sucked in a long breath. "A surprise. Are you fucking crazy?"

Corey stared at her a long moment. "Oh, I have an idea." She pulled out her phone and started searching something.

"Corey." Rachel snapped her fingers. "Focus."

"What?"

"Are you having a stroke?" Rachel gaped at her. "How do you know she even wants to see you?"

"I guess I was hoping you would tell me if she didn't." She shrugged.

"How the hell should I know? All she does is work. I've sent her texts but if I get a response it's just a word, two if I'm lucky."

Corey pursed her lips. "Well, I guess I'll find out then, won't I?" She climbed into her truck, wincing slightly. "Will you lock up for me? I have to roll."

"Wait. How are you going to get this stuff unpacked?" Rachel yelled as she backed out.

"I'll manage. Have fun with Jude."

Corey chewed her lip as she headed out to Thayer's. The only thing she knew for certain was that Thayer was going to be home tonight. As if the hand of God herself had come down to slap some sense into her, Dana had called her out of nowhere that morning and left a message letting her know a new schedule had come out and Thayer was not on it until Monday.

Now Rachel's words rattled around in her head. Maybe she was crazy or having a stroke. Every day for the last two weeks she wanted to call Thayer. It was all she could think about but every day she would find some reason not to. She wasn't ready. She wasn't strong enough. She had an appointment. She wasn't feeling well. She didn't know what to say.

Corey had never had a panic attack but she felt like she was having one now. Her heart raced and her hand sweated on the steering wheel, her breath coming hard and fast. She hit her hazards and pulled over on Old South Road, not three miles from Thayer's house, and prayed no one would drive by.

She rested her head against the steering wheel and wiped her palm against her jeans to dry it, concentrating on slowing her breathing. This all seemed like such a great idea this morning—dinner, drinks, and a heartfelt apology, but now she knew it wasn't enough. How could it ever be enough when Thayer had done nothing wrong? In fact, she had done everything right and

Corey had let her go, pushed her away and rejected her offer of help—rejected her.

"Shit. Shit. Shit." She banged on the steering wheel before throwing open her door and stepping out into the afternoon sun on the desolate road. She needed to pull herself together and get back to the place in her head where she was so sure she could make this right.

The universe wasn't playing around anymore. Everywhere pointed her back to Thayer, every conversation and every thought, but it wasn't until she first met her physical therapist that she was able to get to where she was today, on her way to Thayer's place with steak, chicken, and shrimp ka-bobs that she'd spent all day marinating and awkwardly skewering one-handed.

She'd sat on an exam table in the PT room in the basement of the hospital, not far from the morgue, though she'd never known it was there. She was waiting for whoever was assigned to her case and mindlessly swinging her legs. She stared at a wall with a Henry Ford quote: "Whether you think you can, or you think you can't—you're right."

"Sorry to keep you waiting." A man in his mid-thirties came around the corner and strolled over to Corey, arm extended, a warm smile on his face and a chart tucked under his arm.

Corey assessed him. He was tall and muscular with floppy, sandy-brown surfer hair, a nice tan and two prosthetic legs. She couldn't help but stare and quickly snapped her gaze to his face and shook his hand.

"I'm Dan Lloyd." He saw her eyes flick back to his legs. "I'm a double amputee. Is that going to be a problem?"

"No, of course not. I'm sorry." Corey smiled apologetically. "Corey Curtis and I sleep with women. There, now it's all out in the open."

He grinned. "I do too, and I know who you are. I have to confess there was a bit of a tussle over who was going to work with the Valkyrie."

Corey rolled her eyes. "And you drew the short straw?"

"We fought over your chart, actually. Everyone here has heard what happened and what you did. I can't believe with our workplaces so close we haven't met before, but I wasn't going to miss out on meeting you this time."

"Dan, you said?" Corey started to laugh.

"Yeah, why? What's funny?"

"Nothing. I was just talking to a friend not long ago about not knowing anyone named Dan and here you are." Corey smiled wistfully. "I'm glad it's you."

"So today I just want us to spend some time getting to know each other, talk about your current health and expectations and I'll check you out and see where we are. Sound good?"

"Yeah, great."

Dan set the chart aside. "Take off your shirt for me. Will you be comfortable lying on your stomach on the table? I want to get a look at your back and neck."

Corey pulled her T-shirt over her head, unselfconsciously, though she rarely wore a bra these days because she couldn't get one on. "Yeah, I'll manage." She stretched out and after some fidgeting found an acceptable way to position her cast that didn't aggravate her ribs too much.

"Is that okay?" he asked.

"Yeah, I'm good."

He pressed his fingers into the muscles along her spine and walked his way up, feeling for tension and hot spots. "You may benefit from chiropractic care as well. If you're interested, I can recommend someone really good."

"Great." Corey sighed as he dug his thumbs into the hard muscles of her shoulders and the back of her neck.

"Where do you work out?" Dan manipulated her head carefully back and forth.

It took her a moment to understand the question as whatever he was doing was putting her to sleep. "Uh, Women's MMA Warehouse."

"Oh, yeah." He dug underneath her shoulder blades. "I know it. That place is badass."

"Not doing much fighting these days, but my workouts have been getting better." She sucked in a breath when he hit a particularly tight spot in her neck.

"Sorry." He eased back on the pressure. "How often are you getting headaches?"

"Um, one, two, three in the last ten days, I think."

"Pain scale?"

"Anywhere between three and nine where nine is going blind, throwing up, and passing out."

"That sounds awesome. What's ten then?"

"Being flayed alive, probably."

"Yeah, I get that. You can endure it all when you have to." He continued palpating her back. "What have they been lately?"

"Five or six, I guess."

"Good. And they start in your neck?"

"Yeah, usually. Like tension headaches."

"Yeah, I can feel how tight you are. There are a lot of myofascial trigger points. Your muscles are pulling hard on the right too because you're favoring your left side still. We're going to have to straighten that out and get your posture and gait back to normal. Have you tried massage?"

"Uh, no. I haven't been to anyone."

"Even a nonprofessional would help and I'm sure your girlfriend would know what she was doing better than most."

"Oh, I don't have a girlfriend."

"Oh. What about Dr. Reynolds? Wasn't she there with you?"

"She was, yes." Corey cleared her throat. "But we're not together. I mean we were, maybe, I don't know, but now after everything we're not."

"I've only ever seen her but some of my team have gotten consult requests and taken referrals from her. From what I hear, and believe me pretty much everyone is talking about her, I'd have a hard time believing she couldn't handle what happened. You can sit up." He helped her around on the table and handed her shirt to her. "What happened?"

"She was great. It was me that couldn't handle it."

"Let me guess. You got bitter about what happened to you and the unfairness of it all, and in a fit of raging self-loathing you pushed her away."

Corey laughed humorlessly. "Pretty much nailed it."

"Yeah, I tried that too." Dan nodded. "And?"

"And what?"

"You're just going to let her go? I'm sorry, Corey, and don't get me wrong, because I am a happily married man with baby number two on the way, but if even half of what I've heard about her is true, and a woman like Thayer Reynolds was into me, I'd walk through fire to hold on to that."

She raked her hand through her hair. "Yeah, well I think about it every day and then more time passes and I'm afraid it's too late and I don't know where to start."

He cocked his head and looked at her. "Was she okay after what happened?"

"She wasn't hurt, thank god."

"That's not what I meant. I saw the same news as everyone else. Her life was threatened. That must have been terrifying for her. And she watched you get hurt, yes?"

"Yeah, I guess," she mumbled. "I can't really remember."

"You didn't ask her?"

Corey stared at him, trying to process his words. "No."

"Well, maybe that's where you start." He shrugged. "And, not to sound too cliché, but I'm the guy who got both legs sheared off when I flew off the front of my bike at eighty miles an hour and hit a guardrail." He rapped his knuckles on one of his prosthetics. "It's never too late. Well, unless you're dead— which we are not."

"Right," Corey whispered. "I'm not dead. It's not too late." She took a few deep calming breaths and got in her truck. She had already done so many things wrong. If she turned around now she would regret it for the rest of her life.

CHAPTER THIRTY-TWO

Thayer couldn't believe how exhausted she was, despite leaving the hospital on time—a first for the week. She managed a smile as she thought of her upcoming three days off, though the conversation with her director insisting she take them wasn't something she wanted to repeat.

"Dr. Reynolds, please come in."

Dr. Raymond Manning beckoned her into his office and closed his laptop. He was in his sixties, tall and thin, and she was pretty sure his nickname was Holmes. In all of her previous interactions with him, she had no trouble understanding why. He was well dressed and well-spoken with an air of quiet authority and intelligence.

"You asked to see me?" Thayer was certain she had done nothing wrong and there were no patient complaints about her, but every time she'd been called to the boss's office she felt nervous.

"Please, sit." He gestured to a chair in front of his desk and waited until she was comfortable. "First, let me say how pleased we are that you've joined us at Jackson City Memorial."

"Thank you." Thayer relaxed a little.

"If I may be so bold and ask after your well-being, after everything you and Ms. Curtis endured?" His face showed concern.

Thayer inhaled deeply. "I won't say it hasn't been difficult, but I think I'm doing pretty well. Have there been concerns?"

"On the contrary, I hear nothing but good things about you personally and professionally." He smiled to reassure her. "And Ms. Curtis? I understand she was released some time ago. Is she recovering well?"

Thayer swallowed hard. "I'm sure she is. She's strong."

"Indeed." He nodded. "In our few interactions I've always found her impressive of character."

"She is that, yes." Thayer clamped down hard on her emotions. She didn't want to talk about Corey. "Is there something I can do for you, Dr. Manning?"

"It's what I've done for you," he corrected. "It's come to my attention that you are working far more shifts than is reasonably expected. While I appreciate your dedication to your profession, and specifically this hospital, I would be remiss in my responsibilities as director of this department if I allowed it to continue."

Thayer straightened in her chair and sat forward. "Are you firing me?"

"Good heavens, no. I'm giving you the weekend off." He checked his watch. "Starting right now."

Thayer stared at him. "But it's Thursday."

"A long weekend."

"But I have patients."

"I assure you they will be well taken care of."

"But—"

"I'll see you Monday morning, Dr. Reynolds. The new fourth year transfer is starting and I'm counting on you to show him around." He opened his laptop and shooed her out, his mouth quirking into a small smile.

She was looking forward to picking up her grandmother and bringing her out to the house, planning what they would do in her head. Her smile vanished as she turned down her long drive and saw Corey's truck parked in front of the house. "What the hell?" she muttered but the thump of her heart belied her annoyance.

She didn't see Corey at the front and she didn't have a key, so she had to be in the back. Thayer let herself in, dropped her bag and keys and walked straight to the back, thoroughly pissed off at the feeling of anticipation creeping up on her. She had respected Corey's wishes and stayed away. Now she was here, unannounced and uninvited, but Thayer would be lying to herself if she said she hadn't imagined some version of a reunion like this, and she cursed the hopeless romantic in her.

She pulled open the slider and Corey turned from the grill. A delicious aroma of whatever was cooking made Thayer's stomach rumble. "Corey?"

"Hey." Corey closed the lid, turned the heat down and stepped away from the grill. "How was your day?"

Thayer gaped at her. "How was my day? Is that a joke?" She stepped onto the deck and saw the patio table set for two. There was a wine bottle and a few beers chilling in an ice bucket on one of the benches and Thayer considered guzzling something to settle her nerves. "I haven't heard from you since you left the hospital. Not a call, not a text, nothing. It's been weeks."

"Yeah, um, I guess that was a stupid thing to say." She shuffled her feet, clearly nervous as well.

She surveyed the deck more closely and the amount of work that must have gone into setting it up. "What is all this?"

"Um, a grand gesture?" Corey smiled hopefully. "And an apology…I hope."

Thayer studied her for a long moment, giving herself time to feel what she needed to feel. Her hurt flared to life and with it anger but also a sense of steadiness, pleasure, and hope. She looked Corey over. She stood tall but canted a little to the left, her cast tucked into her side protecting ribs clearly still sore. "How are you?"

Corey met her gaze. "Remorseful. I know I hurt you, Thayer, and I'm sorry."

She understood her motivations, but she fully intended to keep her guard up and be cautious. "We made no promises and you don't owe me anything."

"Actually…" Corey sucked in a deep breath and exhaled. "If I'm remembering correctly I owe you my life."

Thayer gasped softly. "You remember?"

"Some. It's coming back in flashes of bits and pieces. Sometimes I can't hold on to it and it's like trying to remember a dream." She grimaced. "And if I try too hard a raging headache comes on and I end up puking and passing out."

"Oh, Corey." Thayer's heart hurt for her and her resolve to keep her distance began to crack. She wanted to run and wrap her arms around her, but wasn't ready to put herself out there, not yet—not until she knew Corey's intentions. "I'm sorry you got hurt. You have no idea how much."

"I'm getting better. The headaches don't come as often now. I'm seeing a physical therapist and I'm going back to work Monday, restricted duty only, and I've been going to the gym again."

"That's great. What did your neurologist say about the headaches?"

"That it's par for the course." Corey shrugged. "No one really knows with head injuries. Some people never get them, some people wake up and never have another headache, and for some the headaches never go away. You just learn to manage them like every migraine sufferer everywhere."

Thayer nodded. "Should you be driving?"

Corey grinned. "I'm okay to drive. It usually takes time for the migraines to ramp up, and I've learned to predict them pretty well so I can get home if I'm out. One came on instantly and I had to pull over and call Rachel. She found me hurling my guts out on the sidewalk on the way to the grocery store. I almost got arrested for public intoxication."

Thayer didn't know whether to laugh or cry. She was quiet a long time and finally asked, "Why are you here?"

"Because I miss you desperately. Because I was selfish and wrong. All this crazy shit happened to both of us. You lived it too, and you remember it all. I didn't take care of you like you took care of me. I dragged you into this and then bailed in the worst possible way and I never even asked you if you were okay—"

"Stop," Thayer whispered and crossed her arms to cover her trembling hands. She didn't want to think about this. Didn't want to see Corey fall, hear her gasping for air again and fighting to stay conscious. She had packed it all away the same way she did at work after a heartbreaking case.

Corey stepped closer and reached for her. "Thayer."

She stepped away. "Don't." Her voice cracked even on one word as the emotion she had denied choked her. "I just found you and then I thought I lost you." Thayer sucked in a shuddering breath. "But you were going to be okay, and I thought we could heal together and then you just shut me out."

"I know. I'm sorry." Corey moved forward again and Thayer didn't pull away this time. "Thayer, please let me hold you."

She surrendered to her tears as Corey's arm pulled her close. She buried her face in Corey's neck, her body shuddering before relaxing into her as she slipped her arms around Corey's waist and held her tight. "I needed you," she whispered through her tears.

"I'm so sorry." Corey held her tighter.

"Please, don't let me go," Thayer asked simply, unsure whether she meant right this moment or every future moment.

"I won't. Not again."

They held the embrace for a long time, until she felt Corey tense and pulled away, easing her grip around her. "I'm hurting you."

"No." Corey shook her head and smiled to prove it. "It's okay."

Thayer stepped back but held Corey's hand, lacing their fingers together. "So you want to start over?" She brushed tears from her face.

"No." Corey shook her head. "I don't want to pretend the last few weeks didn't happen. It's part of our story. If you'll have me, flaws and all, I would like to pick up where we left off."

Her eyes narrowed in consideration. "What makes you think I haven't moved on?"

Corey's jaw dropped, her eyes going wide. "I, uh, I don't—"

Thayer smiled merrily and kissed the back of Corey's hand. "Oh, honey, you should see your face."

Corey's mouth snapped closed and she shook her head. "That was good."

Her smile turned wicked as she pulled Corey close and slipped her arms carefully around her waist again. "You said where we left off. Don't think I'm going to take it easy on you because you got your brains scrambled."

"Yes, thank you for that." Her right arm came up and draped over Thayer's shoulder.

"And of course I'll have you, flaws and all." She paused to consider. "But I'm not sure if you're quite ready for me to *have you* have you."

"Oh, wait." Corey reached for her phone in her pocket and swiped it on. "One more thing." She tapped the screen and held it over her head as Madonna's "Crazy For You" played.

Thayer's eyes danced with desire. "You remember."

"I was thinking maybe this should be our song," Corey suggested. "You know, if you're into that sort of thing."

She smiled. "I can't think of a better one. I even get your movie reference."

Corey's eyes lit up and she tossed her phone onto the table, the song still playing, and slid her hand around the back of Thayer's neck, pulling her close. "Does that get me laid tonight?"

"Nope." She laughed. "But you're close."

Corey pouted teasingly. "How about we start with a kiss and we can talk over dinner?"

"Yes, please."

Corey's mouth covered hers in a blistering kiss.

CHAPTER THIRTY-THREE

Corey settled Thayer at the table and served her one of each kabob. Corey loved her healthy appetite and spent a full two minutes watching her eat enthusiastically, the best compliment for a chef.

"So, tell me about PT. I know some of the folks down there," Thayer said when she finally took a breath and sat back with her glass of wine.

Corey swallowed her bite and took a sip from her beer, one of two she would allow herself tonight. "His name is Dan Lloyd and he's been really great."

"Dan?" Thayer eyed her. "As in has a truck just like yours, Dan?"

"I thought that was pretty funny too." Corey warmed knowing Thayer quickly recalled one of their earliest interactions. "Within days of seeing him, doing the exercises he recommended, and starting some specific strength training, I really started feeling better and the headaches lessened."

"I'm glad."

"He's been a real mental kick in the ass too."

"How so?"

"He lost both his legs in a motorcycle accident several years ago. He's not big on the self-pity. I needed that."

Thayer twirled her wineglass. "You got pretty dark, huh?"

She thinned her lips. "Rachel told you?"

"She didn't have to." Thayer shrugged. "I was pretty depressed for a while too. Dana recommended a good therapist."

"You've been seeing a therapist?" Her eyes widened and her chest tightened as she realized how little she knew about Thayer's experience with everything that had happened. Her guilt kicked into overdrive.

Thayer looked away. "Corey, I've never been so scared or felt that helpless. I needed to deal with that. I'm still dealing with that."

Corey's heart broke. "I'm so sorry. You could have been killed and I—"

"For you, Corey." Thayer's eyes snapped back to her. "Scared for you. Watching that man attack you. Seeing you fight for your life—our lives. And then seeing you fall…" Her voice broke. "Hearing you land."

"Thayer." Corey closed her eyes briefly.

"I am a healer. It's what I do and who I am. I take care of people all day, many with injuries far more severe than yours, but I never have to watch it happen. It's never been someone I…" She swallowed hard. "…care about. I couldn't reach you. You were in rough shape and there wasn't room for me in the back of the ambulance so I was in front. I couldn't help you, and even when we got to the ED, they wouldn't let me near you for hours. I couldn't do anything. If Dana hadn't been on that night, I think I might've lost my mind."

"Oh, my god," Corey whispered, hanging her head in shame, tears burning behind her eyes. "I didn't know. I didn't ask."

"You weren't supposed to know, and I wouldn't have told you if you'd asked." Thayer reached across the table, opening her hand. "Corey, look at me. You had so many other things to worry about. I didn't want one of them to be me."

"Tell me what I can do," she asked desperately, lacing their fingers together.

After a long silence Thayer whispered, "Stay with me tonight. Be near me. Let me put my head on your chest and listen to your heart and feel you breathe."

The request was so utterly raw and intimate Corey's breath caught. "Yes."

Thayer smiled softly. "I can find you something to sleep in."

Color rushed to her cheeks and she cleared her throat. "That won't be necessary."

Thayer cocked her head, her eyes narrowing. "I'm not getting naked with you tonight."

Her phrasing implied at some later time they would be getting naked. "No, I, um, have some things with me."

Thayer stared at her a long time. "You packed a bag?"

Corey worried she had just ruined their tenuous reunion with her presumptuousness. "Well, I mean—"

"I guess you are on the mend, aren't you?" Thayer's mouth quirked. "Who am I to shatter your fragile new confidence?"

She relaxed and breathed easier. "I appreciate your commitment to my recovery."

"Uh-huh." Thayer's eyes flashed. "Now I have an important question for you and your answer may yet mean doom for us."

"Anything."

Thayer gestured to her cast. "Who the hell is Emma?"

Corey leaned against the pillows in Thayer's bed waiting for her to brush her teeth and finish her bedtime routine. She plucked at her Marvin the Martian pajama pants and black tank, wondering if she should have chosen her sleepwear more carefully. She was still nervous but couldn't yet identify the source of her anxiety.

Thayer leaned in the doorway, eyes smiling. "I think you look terrific."

She looked up and grinned as she took in Thayer's outfit of sweatpants and an oversized long-sleeve shirt. "Um, thanks."

Thayer's eyes narrowed. "Just say it."

Corey fought a laugh. "You will never convince me that's what you normally wear to bed."

"True." Thayer nodded, accepting defeat. "But at the risk of sounding outrageously vain, I didn't want you to get any ideas about what was going to happen tonight."

She barked a laugh. "Thayer, you could be wearing a submarine and I would still get ideas."

Thayer laughed. "Fine." She stripped off the sweats and the shirt hung to mid-thigh. "Better?"

Corey shrugged, secretly wondering what she had on under that shirt. "You're the one who has to sleep in it."

Thayer crawled into bed and stopped nearly a foot from her.

"I will behave, I promise." Corey extended her right arm, encouraging Thayer to move closer.

"I won't hurt you?"

"No." Corey reached for her, tugging on her arm. "But if you do, I probably deserve it."

"What?" Thayer jerked back. "Why would you say that?"

"Nothing. Never mind."

"No, uh-uh, you don't get to do that. Not if you really want this to work. What's going on?"

Corey's face fell, her eyes burning with regret, but she was determined to hold Thayer's gaze. "I feel like I'll never be able to make this up to you. First, getting you involved in my crazy scheme, nearly getting you killed, and then I ruined everything with—"

"Corey, no." Thayer reached for her hand and held it tightly between hers. "I will not let you carry the weight of this any longer. You didn't do this and you have no reason to feel ashamed or guilty. We can talk about how much you remember, and I'll fill in the blanks when you're ready, but I'll tell you this now because I've had to work through this too.

"There were so many things I think I should have done differently. I run it over and over again in my mind, playing out my choices and wondering if I'd refused to go in with you or if I'd fought back. If it was my call to the police that incited him to violence." She sucked in a breath and swallowed hard. "What happened was awful for both of us, but I will not let it define us and I will not let it come between us. Do you hear me?"

"I'm sorry." Her eyes filled, finally spilling over.

Thayer reached to brush her tears away. "You are forgiven, unconditionally. Not that I think you need it, but you seem to need to hear it. That is, officially, the last sorry I will accept from you over this. You did what you felt you had to do to take care of yourself. If our positions had been reversed, I'm not entirely certain I wouldn't have done the same. And look how far you've come? How far both of us have. Now we can go the rest of the way together." She exhaled while Corey remained silent and thoughtful. "Please, say something."

"Thank you," she said, realizing she had never said it, and finally feeling the tight bands of guilt ease from around her chest. She raised her arm again and pulled Thayer next to her.

Thayer shifted, getting comfortable on her side, her head resting in the crook of Corey's arm and her hand covering Corey's heart.

Corey held her close, trying to ignore the heat building in her as Thayer's breasts pressed against her side, the smell of her soap, and the weight of her arm across her chest.

Thayer sighed. "Are you comfortable?"

"Very."

"Are you relaxed?"

"Very."

"Then why is your heart racing?"

"Why is yours?"

Thayer sighed and snuggled closer to her. "Because that's what being near you does to me." Thayer smoothed her hand across Corey's chest.

"Maybe we should talk about your grandmother again?"

"Funny you should mention that." Thayer lifted her head slightly to look at her. "I have a few days off and I was going to pick her up and bring her out tomorrow to spend the day with me. Would you like to meet her?"

"Yes, but I don't want to cut into your time with her."

"Oh, no." Thayer shook her head. "You'd be doing me a favor actually. She already knows about you and has been after me for weeks to bring you by, so seriously, stay here tomorrow and we'll take her out in the boat and fire up the barbeque and work in the garden or something."

"I would love that." Corey smiled and kissed Thayer softly on the mouth.

Thayer settled back down and sighed. "As long as you packed enough clothes, that is."

CHAPTER THIRTY-FOUR

Corey couldn't remember a better weekend. She had an amazing Thursday night with Thayer. They talked, cried, laughed, and held each other. It was intimate in a way she had never experienced and waking up in the morning with Thayer's body curled around her was euphoric.

The next day she spent delightfully with Thayer and Lillian. Unsurprisingly, Thayer's grandmother was a firecracker telling stories of her years at the lake and embarrassing Thayer at every chance. Corey laughed at Thayer's mortification when her grandmother went into great detail about an article she'd read on the latest in artificial reproductive technology and same sex couples. They had hugged each other fiercely when they drove back to her residence Friday night.

And now they were throwing an impromptu Saturday girls' night at Corey's condo. Thayer suggested it be their coming out party and the official announcement of their relationship. Their friends had been polite and respectful in their inquisitions—except for Rachel—but both Corey and Thayer felt they owed them thanks for all of their support and encouragement.

Corey was feeling the strain of the last couple of days, both physically and emotionally, as she and Thayer found their way back to each other, but she pushed through. She had been hiding long enough and it was time to put herself back out there.

They were rushing now, unpacking groceries and getting out the margarita glasses. The girls would be over any minute for dinner and drinks and game night. Even though Corey and Thayer had just reunited, when they discovered all their friends had the same weekend night off, they couldn't let the opportunity to get everyone together pass by. They had all crossed paths frequently while Corey was in the hospital, but this would be the first official social event, and Corey and Thayer both pretended they wouldn't rather be cuddling on Corey's sofa watching movies.

Corey turned, a bottle of mix in her hand. "Damn it, I forgot the limes."

"It's fine." Thayer preheated the oven for the enchiladas they had made earlier, poured chips into a bowl and opened a jar of salsa. "No one drinks margaritas for the lime."

"I can run back. I can…get…get…" Corey stuttered and hissed a breath, the bottle sliding from her hand and shattering on the kitchen floor in a spray of glass and mix. "No. No. Not now." She gritted her teeth and wavered, her right hand going to the back of her neck and her cast banging down on the counter to steady herself.

"Corey!" Thayer skirted the mess and rushed to her, getting an arm around her waist before she collapsed.

"What do you need?"

"Help me upstairs." Her voice was tight, her eyes closed to slits with pain, white-hot and relentless.

Thayer took her weight as they moved awkwardly through Corey's condo and upstairs to her room. She eased her down on the bed and asked, "Where are your meds?"

"Bathroom." Corey doubled over, gulping breaths and wrapping both arms across her middle.

Thayer flung open the medicine cabinet and grabbed the bottles and a glass of water.

From downstairs she could hear Rachel and Cin talking worriedly about the mess in the kitchen. They must have let themselves in. "Here." She gently opened Corey's hand and gave her the meds.

Corey got them in her mouth with a trembling hand and reached for the glass Thayer knew she wouldn't be able to hold. She sat on the bed next to her, holding the glass to her lips, one hand against the back of her neck to steady her. She could feel the muscles in Corey's neck, rigid with spasm and no doubt excruciating. Corey closed her eyes and curled into a tight ball.

"Oh, sweetheart." Thayer's heart clenched in sympathy seeing her in so much pain. She got behind her and kneeled on the bed, placing her hands on Corey's shoulders, her thumbs easing into her rock-hard muscles. Corey groaned against the pressure.

"Shhh," Thayer whispered. "It's okay. Let me help." She kneaded Corey's muscles, her shoulders, neck, and base of her head, slowly beginning to feel them ease their attack. She sensed another presence in the room and turned to the door to see Rachel, looking worried.

"Do you need anything?" Rachel asked quietly, having helped Corey through more than her share over the last few weeks.

"Can you draw the shades and hit the lights?" She pressed her thumbs into the base of Corey's head, the spot that seemed to provide the most relief. "I'll be down in a few minutes."

Thayer felt her slip into sleep, her body finally relaxing and the tension leaving her face. She massaged her neck for a few more minutes until she heard her snoring softly.

Thayer climbed off the bed and flexed her fingers. She straightened Corey's legs and arranged her into a more comfortable position. She placed a soft kiss on her cheek before covering her with the blanket and heading back downstairs.

Corey padded downstairs several hours later, bleary-eyed and still dopey. Her living room was alive with raucous laughter as Cin refilled drinks from a pitcher of margaritas.

"Hey, Cor, how are you feeling?" Rachel hopped out of the armchair to let her have it and moved to the floor next to Jules.

"Better, thanks." She rubbed her eyes and gratefully accepted the bottle of water Cin grabbed from the kitchen. She could feel Thayer's concerned eyes on her and smiled in her direction. "What did I miss?"

She was disappointed to have missed their gathering, but she and Thayer had come to an agreement the other night. If they were going to give their relationship a chance and see where it went, Corey wouldn't hide from her—no matter what—and Thayer wouldn't stop her life or do anything different, thinking she had to take care of her, no matter what. Corey was pleased to see, Thayer keeping up her end. For her part, though, she couldn't remember anything during the migraine attack, but she was pretty sure Thayer got the full frontal. At least she didn't throw up.

"Well, I killed it in Cards Against Humanity," Dana said smugly and sat back with her drink.

"I fucking hate that game," Corey mumbled.

"Since when are you so delicate?" Cin chided. "It's supposed to be offensive."

"It's not that. It's just so clearly made by dudes. I mean if there was a single woman writing those cards, there'd be cards about period farts or cervical mucus."

They all gaped at her before roaring in drunken laughter.

"That's nasty." Jules giggled.

"Oh, but a card about smegma isn't?" Corey went on.

They laughed harder.

Thayer eyed her. "How high are you right, now?"

"Oh, yeah, Thayer doesn't know yet that after a headache Corey has no inner monologue for like a day." Rachel winked at Cin.

"Totally," Cin agreed enthusiastically. "It's like truth serum. If you want to know her deepest and darkest, now is the time."

"Oh, really?" Thayer grinned at her. "Well, as fun as that sounds, I'll probably try not to take advantage of her in her weakened condition." A chorus of good-natured boos followed.

"Aw, thanks, babe," Corey replied and immediately clamped her mouth shut. From the look of surprise on both their faces that term of endearment was new to them both.

The four other women descended into gales of laughter and Thayer blushed, eying Corey from behind her drink.

"Shit." Corey sighed and raked her hands through her hair sticking it up, grinning sheepishly at her.

Jules recovered first. "So, Corey, can I ask something?" She went on without waiting for an answer. "When I was in nursing school, I was thinking of specializing in neurology. I did some research on traumatic brain injury and long-term effects. Is there something that triggers your headaches?"

Corey blew out a breath. She had just been talking about this with Thayer. "Sometimes nothing but more often than not, they happen when I'm physically active or I'm hyperemotional, for lack of a better way to describe it."

Rachel choked on her drink. "Like the Hulk?"

"Sure, exactly like that, except instead of turning into a badass superhero, I cry and vomit until I pass out because it feels like someone is sticking an ice pick through the back of my skull." She meant to be funny but from the silence in the room she could tell it hadn't worked.

"I mean, it's not just when you're angry," Jules said.

"No. Tonight, for example. I was really looking forward to you guys coming over and I've been pretty busy the last couple of days." Her eyes flicked to Thayer. "I guess I tripped the breaker."

"Wait. Wait." Rachel held up her hands. "Physical activity and excitement? Any emotion?" She looked between Corey and Thayer whose expressions said they both knew where this conversation was going. "What happens when you two—"

"I wouldn't know." Corey looked pointedly at Thayer. "The doctor is definitely not in."

"What?" Dana blurted, her eyes narrowing at Thayer. "But you told me you couldn't wait to get Corey—"

"Okay," Thayer cut her off. "We don't need to discuss—"

"Oh, yes, we do," Cin chimed in, alcohol fueling everyone's interest. "So, no sexual healing, for real?"

Corey laughed and stared at Thayer. "Well?" She held up her cast and waggled her fingers when Thayer stayed stubbornly silent. "She claims it's my busted arm and sore ribs, but I bet Thayer thinks so highly of herself she's worried she's going to blow my mind and put me in a coma."

Thayer stared back at her, shaking her head and fighting a smile as the others erupted into laughter again. "That's very funny."

"Clearly." Corey smirked and gestured to the others still cackling.

"All right, enough." Thayer buried her reddening face in her hands. "I confess, Corey has pulled out all the stops." She glanced Corey's way to see her grinning like a fool. "But, and I admit it's getting more difficult, I have successfully shut her down." The resounding boos and laughter went on for a long time.

"Because." Thayer had to yell over the din. "Because yes, I am concerned about her, ahem, overexerting herself." The laughter escalated. Thayer was laughing now too. "And I have a vested interest in seeing that for our first time, and for that matter, every subsequent time, we are both in peak form." Thayer grinned at them. "I have standards and a reputation to protect."

The laughter died away and their friends seemed to consider her last words.

"That's fair," Rachel agreed.

"Yeah, never settle," Jules piped up.

"I totally get that," Cin added.

"Hey," Corey blurted and looked to Dana who was hiding her laughter behind a long drink. "What the hell?"

CHAPTER THIRTY-FIVE

After showing the last of their friends out, Corey leaned against the door, wearily. "They stayed late." It was after midnight when the party started breaking up and the ladies helped clean up and called cabs since no one was fit to drive.

Thayer wrapped her arms around Corey's waist and laid her head on her shoulder. "They wanted to spend time with you."

"Yeah, that sucked. I'm sorry."

"For what?" Thayer's head snapped up and she placed a hand on the side of Corey's face, stroking her cheek. "New rule. Don't ever apologize to me when you don't feel well or you need help, okay?"

"Okay." Corey smiled and placed a soft kiss on Thayer's lips, her arm going around her back. "Are you staying?" They were still so new Corey didn't want to assume anything.

"Would you like me to?" Thayer kissed her again, deeper and longer and pressed herself against the length of Corey's body.

"Yes." Corey sighed into the kiss, feeling the first stirrings of arousal. She tipped her head and brushed her lips along Thayer's neck and down lower to trace her collarbone, nipping lightly at the sensitive skin of her throat.

"Oh." Thayer shivered, dropping her head back as Corey worked her way along her throat and back up to her mouth, teasing her tongue along her bottom lip before covering Thayer's mouth with her own.

Corey dragged the kiss out, slowly and hotly. She could feel Thayer respond, pressing against her, hands digging into her back through her shirt, soft moans of pleasure deep in her throat. "Thayer," Corey breathed, nipping at her bottom lip with her teeth and smiling at her sharp hiss of breath.

"Mmm?"

"I'm exhausted." Corey pulled away abruptly, a wicked smile on her face. "I'm heading up. Will you get the lights?"

Thayer stared at her, lips parted, eyes bright with arousal. "What?" She licked her lips, and smiled in defeat. "That's very clever."

"Suffer woman," Corey called from the stairs. "You deserve it."

Corey sighed, her eyes fluttering open as a teasing hand slipped beneath her T-shirt and traced the planes of her belly and along her sides. She sucked in a sharp breath as fingertips brushed the side of her breast. "Thayer," she gasped, her body coming alive at the touch. "What are you doing?"

"Shhh," Thayer whispered, her fingertips tickling across Corey's breast, hardening a nipple.

Corey's hand shot up, gripping Thayer's wrist, stopping her. "Don't you dare start something you're not going to finish."

"Don't worry. I'll finish you. Eventually."

Corey let go of her wrist, her gaze steady on her. "What does that mean?"

"It means, you stay still and let me do all the work." Thayer slid her fingers across Corey's chest, slowly circling her other breast. "If I think you're in pain, in ways I don't intend, I'll stop. If you cannot agree to my terms, I'll stop now."

Corey groaned, her heart thudding in her chest and her muscles contracting as Thayer skimmed her fingers down her belly and slipped them along the inside of her waistband. "Your terms are acceptable."

"You say that now." Thayer leaned over and sealed their deal with a searing kiss before straddling Corey's hips. She watched her carefully as she settled herself. "Good?"

Corey's eyes were hooded with desire, her nipples hardening at the sight of Thayer astride her in a T-shirt and panties. "Good."

Thayer slipped her hands beneath Corey's shirt, her palms sliding against her skin as she eased it over her head and past her cast. "Your body is simply incredible. You're so beautiful and so strong," Thayer murmured, running her hands down Corey's chest, swirling her palms over her breasts, hardening her nipples further. She smoothed her palms down her abdomen. Corey's taut muscles jumped and bunched beneath her touch.

Corey's lips parted, sucking in a panting breath. "Oh, god." Blood roared in her ears, her arousal aching against Thayer's weight over her.

"Shhh. Breathe. I don't want to have to stop." Thayer smiled down at her. "I like you like this—ready and wanting." She took Corey's right hand, lacing their fingers together and pressing her arm into the bed by her head, holding her there as she bent, raining hot kisses along her neck, working her way slowly up to her lips.

Corey accepted her kisses, hungrily. Thayer controlled their pace as her tongue darted in and out, tasting her. Then she moved on, trailing wet kisses down the other side of Corey's neck.

Thayer stopped and sat back again, surveying her work. Corey was flushed, a fine sheen of sweat breaking out across her face and chest. "Are you all right?"

Corey nodded, swallowing hard several times. "Yes."

"Okay." Thayer adjusted Corey's cast comfortably away from her side and out of the way. "Stay still, now." She waited for Corey's nod of acknowledgment before pulling her own shirt over her head, sitting back in only her panties.

Corey's lips parted, her eyes widening as Thayer revealed herself. Her smooth, bronze skin, full, round breasts with soft brown nipples, and a firm, toned body elicited a desperate groan.

"You'll get your turn." Thayer grinned. "Maybe later." She leaned over Corey and kissed her once more on the mouth before trailing hot kisses down her chest and sucking one nipple hard into her mouth.

Corey arched as Thayer's teeth held her firmly. "Shit."

"Easy," Thayer commanded as she released her and kissed her way over to the other breast, lavishing the nipple with tongue and teeth. "I don't want you to get too excited."

Corey breathed a laugh. "Don't forget," she gasped as Thayer kissed her way down her body again, circling her navel with her tongue while sliding her hands over her breasts, kneading them both. "What comes around goes around."

Thayer grinned around her kisses. "Why don't you let me worry about who's coming and when."

Corey tensed when Thayer slipped her fingers beneath the waistband of Corey's shorts and slid them down over her hips. Thayer's taunting words and tortuous lovemaking had her on fire, her core molten and heavy with need. Corey no longer believed she was doing this only out of concern. She knew Thayer was enjoying her control and the razor's edge she was leading her slowly toward.

Corey was naked now, exposed and painfully aroused as Thayer hovered over her, not touching her but letting her eyes roam her body, as if deciding where to go next. "I've been dreaming of this since the moment I first saw you."

Corey groaned, squirming under her gaze. Her lovers before, though not many, had always appreciated her body but none had worshipped her the way Thayer was, with slow strokes over every inch of skin. Her gaze was so intense, Corey was almost self-conscious. Her need for her was stoked higher with every teasing touch. "Didn't your dream involve this happening faster?" She gasped as Thayer's fingers brushed through her damp curls and cupped her.

"Oh, I have a dream for that too," Thayer assured her and slid one finger through Corey's slick center. "I have a very healthy imagination." She pushed against Corey's thighs encouraging her to spread her legs. "But given your current physical condition I've opted for the slow dream."

She sucked in a sharp breath, hips jerking as Thayer touched her again, slender fingers parting her and circling her aching center. "My current...current condition is critical." Her breath hitched as Thayer toyed with her.

"I want to taste you." Thayer's eyes glittered as she lowered her mouth to Corey's belly and kissed her way down, teasing the sensitive skin with her tongue and teeth.

She panted, her body on fire, as Thayer spread her legs further. She could feel herself opening in anticipation as Thayer nestled her face between her legs. "Oh, god." She choked as Thayer's hot mouth closed over her, licking, lapping, and sucking. Her hips surged into her, searching desperately for the pressure she needed. She was so close and Thayer hummed her approval.

Corey felt tears pricking behind her eyes. She was so overwhelmed with sensation and need. Even if she wanted to move she couldn't. She was paralyzed, her body liquid under Thayer's unrelenting attention. "Thayer...please..."

Thayer grinned around her, taking her fully into her mouth one more time before gathering herself and sliding a hand up Corey's leg, her fingers parting her again. "I want to watch you come," she whispered as she slid two fingers gracefully inside her.

Corey's mouth dropped open in a silent cry as Thayer filled her, stroking her contracting walls. She couldn't catch her breath as Thayer's hand slid smoothly in and out, searching for the perfect rhythm.

Corey groaned when Thayer's thumb pressed down on her hard center, her hips matching Thayer's pace as her climax built from her belly, radiating out in liquid heat as she came with the force of two suns colliding.

She arched from the bed, crying out Thayer's name as she continued to stroke her through the longest most powerful orgasm of her life until she collapsed back on the bed totally senseless.

Her eyes fluttered a moment later and Thayer's perfect breasts swam into view over her face. "Am I in heaven?"

"Shhh." Thayer still straddled her, leaning over to massage her neck and shoulders. "Lie still and breathe. I don't want you to tighten up."

"Tighten up?" Corey smiled slowly. "I can't feel my legs. I've never been this relaxed in my life," she laughed.

Thayer sat back on Corey's hips and eyed her carefully. "You feel okay?"

She felt like she'd taken a hit of nitrous gas, as she had in college, her smile sloppy and her body detached. "Marvelous."

Thayer breathed a sigh. "Okay, good."

Corey felt the delicious tingle between her legs and still jerked as aftershocks rolled through her. "Morning sex is the best sex." She sighed.

Thayer smiled and ran her hands up Corey's chest as she leaned down to give her a tender kiss. "We are in accord."

Corey's eyes widened. "But you wanted dinner first."

Thayer's mouth quirked as she relaxed back on her heels across her hips. "I ate with the girls last night."

"And multiple orgasms."

"I took care of that last night before I came upstairs. On your sofa by the way."

Corey gaped at her. "You did not."

"I did so." Thayer laughed. "What? You never masturbate?"

"Oh no, I do." Corey pursed her lips. "Quite often since I met you, in fact."

Thayer eyed her. "Do I have a role in your masturbatory fantasies?"

"You, in fact, play the lead in all of them."

"How many are there?"

I have a healthy imagination too." Corey grinned and slid her right hand up Thayer's thigh and brushed her fingers across panties so damp they were now transparent.

"Tell me," Thayer whispered.

Corey gripped her hip and tugged gently. "If you get naked right now and sit forward a bit, I'll gladly show you. This one might be my favorite."

In an unprecedented act of flexibility Thayer stripped out of her soaked panties, laughing at Corey's dumbfounded expression. "Yoga."

"Thanks be to yoga." Corey pulled her forward.

Thayer frowned. "I'll hurt you."

"No, you won't."

She moved forward and lowered herself over Corey's belly, her glistening auburn curls tickling Corey's navel.

Corey's breath hitched as she adjusted to her weight and felt Thayer's damp heat against her skin. "Perfect." She could reach up with her good arm and cup Thayer's breast, feeling the glorious weight of her. "You are so gorgeous. I wish I had a better word." She kneaded first one breast and then the other.

"You don't need words. Show me." Thayer arched her back into her hand and sighed with pleasure as Corey's thumb circled her nipples hardening them. "Oh, that's good."

Corey felt her shudder as she played with her breasts. She enjoyed breast play, and to her delight, Thayer was incredibly sensitive. She filed that away for when she had use of both hands again.

Thayer's hips swirled down on her, seemingly of their own accord, as Corey touched her breasts, belly, and inner thigh. She slid her hand between them curling into her slick folds. Thayer allowed Corey in, her fingers teasing open her hot center.

Thayer gasped, her eyes flying open to meet Corey's heated gaze as she lowered herself onto her hand with a husky moan. "Oh, god, Corey." She growled as Corey's hand sank deeper into her.

She was wet and her ready walls contracted around Corey's fingers. "You're so hot."

"For you." Thayer swirled again, her lids fluttering closed.

Corey let Thayer lead as her fantasy involved Thayer being a recklessly uninhibited lover. She was not disappointed. Thayer rocked against her hand, raising and lowering herself at will, and at times, impaling herself so deep Corey feared she might break her other arm.

The most erotic sounds Corey had ever heard erupted from Thayer as she ground down on her, eyes locked on Corey the entire time.

Thayer smiled languidly and ran her own hands across her body, sliding them up to knead her own breasts and tease her nipples to impossible points.

Corey gasped at the sight, her arousal spiking again, painfully, and cursing her useless left hand, desperate to be the one touching Thayer's perfect breasts.

"Corey," Thayer gasped, her eyes glassy and unseeing as her climax neared. "I'm so close."

She ground down hard, Corey wincing at the twinge in her ribs as Thayer lost control, throwing her head back and crying out her pleasure. Her hips bucked against Corey's hand until she swayed and dropped forward, boneless, her mass of untamed curls tickling Corey's chest.

"Thayer," Corey squeaked, pushing against her shoulder with her cast hand, her right still buried deep inside her.

"Oh shit." Thayer's head popped up and she adjusted her weight, easing herself from Corey's hand with a gasp. "Are you okay? I'm so sorry. Did I hurt you?"

"No. I'm fine." She inhaled deeply. "It's fine."

Thayer stretched out on Corey's good side, snuggling into the crook of her arm, her hair fanned out against her chest. "I like your dreams too," she said lazily, draping an arm across her chest.

Corey trailed her fingers across Thayer's back. "Remind me, what's next on your list?"

"A shower," Thayer purred.

"Right." Corey sighed contentedly. "Now or later?"

Thayer trailed her fingertips down Corey's side. "Later. Much later."

EPILOGUE

Corey practically skipped into the ED, her mood soaring. Her relationship with Thayer, the most beautiful woman inside and out that Corey had ever known, had bloomed over the last few weeks into the kind of love she thought only existed in movies and trashy romance novels. Her heart beat faster, her smile grew, and her body tingled every time she saw her. Thayer was warm, caring, funny, and smart. She challenged Corey and never failed to call her out on her shit. She was an adventurous lover who made Corey feel like the sexiest woman alive.

The transition back to her life had not been without its problems. Corey's headaches ramped back up as soon as she started back to work. She immediately thought it was chemical exposure, even at safe low levels, and she tried wearing a respirator all day. It was awkward, uncomfortable, and ultimately unsustainable and she was devastated that her job was at stake. Also, it was not the problem.

It was Thayer who suggested the hospital's fluorescent lights were the culprit. It was common for migraines to be triggered by harsh lighting and even Thayer felt the eye strain after a long shift.

After a little bit of research they selected yellow tinted glasses designed specifically to reduce effects of certain light wavelengths. The results were dramatic and immediate and Corey bounced back again with a vengeance.

The mystique surrounding the Valkyrie had already been elevated to outlandish levels with what had happened. Now Corey sported lightly tinted wraparound shades all day and was much more visible due to her relationship with Thayer. Thayer teased her often about the oglers she attracted with her new look, which had Corey completely baffled. She didn't mind that Thayer found her that much more alluring and they had a near-miss *Grey's Anatomy* elevator moment as a result. Thayer was so mortified that they established their own no canoodling at work rule. They did manage to occasionally steal alone time in the morgue, which they both agreed was way sexier than it had any right to be.

She grinned goofily, her eyes darting around the ED, passing over the dozens of faces but not finding Thayer. Her face fell and she strode to the desk, her cast clunking down on the counter hard enough to make Dana jump, her attention torn from the phone at her ear and the stack of charts splayed out in front of her.

"Corey what the hell?" Dana hissed, covering her hand over the mouthpiece.

"Is she here?" Corey was oblivious to Dana's annoyance.

"Hold on a sec," she said into the phone before turning her attention to her. "Of course she's here. Maybe you haven't noticed we're slammed this morning."

The waiting room was brimming with people and all the triage beds were full, doctors and nurses hustling between them, heads bent over charts or deep in consultation with one another.

Corey sighed in frustration but tried not to whine. "She said she'd cut my cast off today if I came up first thing."

"And I'm sure she will when she has time."

"But—"

"Is it an emergency?"

"No, but—"

"Then be patient. No pun intended." Dana waved her off and went back to her call.

Corey grunted her displeasure and turned in time to see Thayer crossing the hall, jotting notes in a chart. The morning sun streaming through the window behind her caught the highlights in her hair, making it appear as if she were glowing.

She sucked in a breath at her beauty and the way she carried herself with such confidence and poise. She was positively stunning and Corey never failed to take notice.

Thayer must have felt the heat of her stare. She stopped and looked up, a smile lighting up her face.

Corey smiled back and held up her cast arm.

Thayer's gaze flicked to it and her smile faltered. "I can't now. I'm sorry," she mouthed.

Corey couldn't hide her disappointment.

Thayer frowned and checked her watch. "Half hour?"

"Dr. Reynolds?" Two voices called for her simultaneously from opposite ends of the hall.

Thayer waved regretfully at Corey and disappeared in the direction of the one closest to her.

Corey's shoulders drooped and she looked down at her cast, filthy and stinking after more than six weeks. "Fuck you, you bastard," she muttered and stalked off.

She banged open the morgue door and crossed to the counter jerking open a drawer with a clattering of the steel instruments inside. She yanked out the Stryker saw and held it up, laughing maniacally.

She put on a fresh blade. It was a bone saw and she had no idea if it would cut fiberglass but she intended to find out. She set her arm up on the counter and flipped the switch, the saw whirring to life.

She was almost down to her elbow, the blade whining its way through her cast, when she caught motion by the door.

She looked up to see Thayer leaning against the jamb, amusement flashing in her golden eyes. She switched off the saw smiling guiltily.

"You are determined and resourceful."

Corey shrugged. "Sorry."

"I'm surprised you didn't do it sooner."

"Didn't occur to me until just now or I would have."

"Show me how it works." Thayer took the saw from her.

"Just hit the switch in the back."

"Is it safe?" Thayer turned it on. "Oh, it vibrates not rotates."

"It won't cut skin." Corey assured her, and much to her surprise and delight, with total trust, Thayer immediately touched her thumb to the blade.

She jumped, startled at the sensation and examined her unharmed skin. "Huh. That's cool." She placed the saw into the split Corey had already started. "Let's do this."

Corey grinned, ridiculously, and in only a few minutes Thayer cracked the cast off. Corey groaned when she extended her arm for the first time in more than six weeks and ripped off the gauze and cotton padding, itching her flaky, pale, skin.

Thayer laughed at her dramatic display of relief.

"Oh, fuck that feels so good."

"Let me see." Thayer reached for her and held her hand. "Squeeze."

"I feel so weak."

"That's to be expected after total immobilization for that long." She turned her arm around in her hand and smoothed a hand along her visibly thinner arm. "Your muscles have atrophied some. But for you that only means you have the left arm strength of a mere mortal. Any pain?"

"No, but, Jesus, my arm needs a sandwich."

"Just keep doing what you do and you'll be back to you in no time. Are you still seeing Dan?"

"Tomorrow. He's already signed off on the paperwork so I can go back on full duty." She was no longer looking at her arm but staring at Thayer's lips, full and glistening lightly with the vanilla gloss she favored.

"What?" Thayer smiled at her curiously.

"I'm crazy in love with you," she blurted.

Thayer's brows shot to her hairline and she stared at her, speechless.

Corey's eyes widened when she realized what she'd just said. "I'm sorry."

Thayer's expression softened, her golden eyes warming with emotion. "Why? Did you not mean it?"

She winced. "I didn't mean to say it for the first time in the morgue."

"I don't care where you say it as long as you say it often and for a very long time." Thayer stepped closer and slid her arms around Corey's neck. "Put your arms around me."

She did and pulled her close. "I'm in love with you, Thayer Reynolds."

Thayer brushed her lips over hers. "I know."

Corey jerked away from her, surprised.

Thayer winked. "See what I did there?"

"That's very funny, Han. I'm relieved I don't need to include any *Star Wars* in your film education." Corey laughed, pulling her close again and covering her mouth, kissing her long and deep.

In anticipation of getting her cast off, Corey had brought in fifteen-pound dumbbells and was struggling through her third set of biceps curls with her left arm when Cin burst in through the door, eyes bright and face flushed with excitement.

Corey straightened and shook her arm out. "What the hell has gotten into you?"

"Good, you're here," Cin said somewhat breathlessly as she breezed by her and into the autopsy room. She flung open the bottom cabinets and started stacking items onto the counter— shoe covers, hooded Tyvek suits, sleeves, gloves, safety glasses, face shields, biohazard bags, and towels.

"What's going on?" Corey leaned in the doorway, curious. "Is it the apocalypse?"

"Audrey got a call this morning from JCPD about assisting on a recovery," Cin explained as she packed up all her supplies in one of the biohazard bags and ducked into another cabinet for the portable LED lights. Audrey Marsh, the university's forensic anthropologist, always got called for skeletal remains and the examination took place in her lab on campus.

"So, you thought you'd raid my shit?" Corey asked. "What do you need all that for, anyway? How old are the bones?"

"Not bones," Cin replied. "A decomp."

"Yuck." Corey grimaced. "So, that's what I have to look forward to tomorrow? Wait, why is Dr. Marsh doing it?"

"The body is severely decomposed and not able to be identified or autopsied, most likely. It's still unclear how it's all going to work. Audrey has been talking to Dr. Webster and the police. I think it's going to be a joint effort."

Corey perked up at the idea of assisting Audrey Marsh, her old professor and advisor, on a forensic case. "Where's the body?"

Cin's phone chimed a text message. "That's Aud with the location now." She was halfway through the door when she turned back to Corey. "You're not coming?"

"Am I invited?" Corey asked, her face brightening.

"Yeah, did you miss the part where I said joint effort?" Cin jerked her head out the door. "Hurry up. Aud is waiting for us and we're going to need to grab scrubs on the way out. Hey, you got your cast off."

Corey couldn't contain her grin as she grabbed her keys and phone from the desk and followed Cin out. "Totally cut it off with the Stryker."

"What's Thayer going to say about that?"

Corey's smile widened. "Thayer helped."

Cin laughed at her. "Wow, your face right now…"

"What?"

"Nothing. You just look really happy." Cin nodded to her phone. "You need to message and let her know you're on a field trip?"

"Better not," she replied. "Pretty sure Thayer won't thank me for getting her involved in another one of my cases."

Bella Books, Inc.

Women. Books. Even Better Together.

P.O. Box 10543
Tallahassee, FL 32302

Phone: 800-729-4992
www.bellabooks.com

9 781642 470079